RIDING
CHANCE

CHRISTINE KENDALL

Scholastic Press / New York

All rights reserved. Published by Scholastic Press, an imprint of Scholastic Inc., *Publishers since 1920.* SCHOLASTIC, SCHOLASTIC PRESS, and associated logos are trademarks and/or registered trademarks of Scholastic Inc.

Library of Congress Cataloging-in-Publication Data available

ISBN 978-0-545-92404-7

10 9 8 7 6 5 4 3 2 1   16 17 18 19 20

Printed in the U.S.A.   23
First edition, October 2016

Book design by Mary Claire Cruz

For Mitchell, with love

CHAPTER ONE

SEE, THE FLOW'S THE THING. You know, we all got our swagger when we're on the block. Don't take no stuff from the fellas, profiling for the ladies. Well, same thing when I'm up on that horse. I got my moves and my horse got hers. It's the flow that first grabbed me.

It sure wasn't what I expected. After what happened, me and my boy Foster were just trying to keep it all together. Especially me. I was messed up—confused pretty bad—but I couldn't tell anybody. Not Foster, not my family, nobody.

"Mr. Butler." The social worker folded her hands on her desk and leaned toward Pops. "Our prevention program has your son's name written all over it." I didn't know what she was trying to prevent. My mom had already died and, after that, it felt like I was living in a tunnel. Even when I was outside on a sunny day, everything still felt dark.

Pops sighed real deep and shook his head. "Everything used to be fine," he said. It must have been hard for him to hear what all I'd been doing—skipping school, hanging out with knuckleheads. He'd had to take time off from work for this. "Maybe this will help him get back on track."

I squeezed my eyes shut and swallowed hard. They didn't know the half of it. They didn't know that I was there when that old man got mugged, when Lay-Lay took his forty bucks. Foster was smart enough to back away from that, but not me. *Troy, Lay-Lay's bad news, man.* That's exactly what Foster said. Maybe I didn't listen 'cause I was still feeling like I was underwater. You know how when you're in the big swimming pool at the Y? Holding your breath, you can't hear everything that's going on around you. That's how I was feeling.

"Well," the social worker said, "in light of the iPhones incident—"

"We didn't steal them," I broke in, "we were just holding them . . ." I was still trying to figure out how we got punished for what Lay-Lay did, but nobody wanted to hear it.

The social worker held up her hand. "We're in agreement with the police, Mr. Butler. Troy and his friend Foster would benefit from our program."

I guess that was the cops' way of saying we weren't hard-core or nothing, so they sent us to talk to this lady about working with horses in the park. My first thought was, what's that got to do with me? I didn't know nothing about horses, didn't wanna know nothing about horses, and didn't nobody I know play with horses.

"Sounds like a good idea," said Pops. "Troy's been under a lot of stress lately."

I almost laughed. Stress. Is that what it's called when you lose the person you love the most? I didn't know what to say, but when I looked over at Pops, I didn't see any brightness in his eyes. He was still struggling, too. How could I say no to messing around with some horses?

Pops didn't have much to say on the ride home. Used to be he'd put on some jazz and try to explain the music to me. But right then, he was quiet. Totally quiet, like our house was most of the time. I couldn't stand everything being so dark and hushed, so I went over to Foster's crib.

I liked hanging out over there 'cause his mom had made their place funky, not like our house. There were candles and incense in the living room, and Foster had a parachute attached to the ceiling of his bedroom. Felt like we were sitting in a tent or something. It was our clubhouse.

"Aw, man, I don't believe you," I said, looking over his shoulder. "You're looking up horses?"

"I've never seen one up close." My boy always did his research. He shifted his body to the right to hide his computer screen from me. "Listen to this. A horse is a plant-eating animal . . ."

"Horses don't eat meat?" I leaned over to his left side and saw this mad picture of an all-black horse running on a beach. Foam from the ocean waves was bubbling around the horse's feet, and its hair was flowing straight back from its long neck. "Other than the beach thing, looks like me on the ball court," I said, nudging his shoulder.

"You wish," he said, waving me off.

Foster lets me talk a lot of trash. He knows it's just my way of dealing with everything. He got into trouble because of me but he never threw that in my face. Now he was looking up stuff so it'd look like we knew something when we got there. "What's that game the social worker was talking about?" he asked. He was working his way through more pictures. "Some sport you can play if you're good on a horse?"

"Polo," I said. "I thought it was just a designer shirt."

"Here it is." Foster clicked through a few websites. "Polo: a high-speed game played on horseback." He pushed his chair away from his desk so I could see a picture of a guy dressed all fly on a horse and holding a long stick. "Looks stupid if you ask me."

"Man, this whole thing is stupid," I said. I threw myself down on Foster's beanbag and looked up at his parachute. Felt like I'd been thrown out of an airplane without one. Lay-Lay set us up. There was no question about that. I squeezed my eyes shut for a few seconds; sometimes that helped me to not feel so confused. "Well, at least we'll be out in the park."

"Working for free," Foster added.

"We can just fake it," I said. "Nobody will know the difference."

CHAPTER TWO

GROWING UP IN PHILLY, I'd been used to going to Fairmount Park. We did all kinds of stuff, like barbecues in the summer, haunted house tours at Halloween. Me and Foster used to ride our bikes in the park, too, popping wheelies and looking at girls.

Some days when I didn't go to school, I'd take real long walks in the park. It's beautiful no matter what season it is. What I liked the most is that I could be alone there, especially when it was cold and there weren't any leaves on the trees. Maybe I needed that because I felt exposed like the bare tree branches. Even under my winter coat and hat and gloves. It seemed like I walked all over the park that winter, but the park's so big, I guess you can never get to know all of it.

Now it was spring and these horse people took us to a place we'd never been before. Everything was green, and the leaves were budding on the tall trees all around the stables. There was a red barn and it sat real low, almost in the ground, slurping up mud on its sides. Mostly brick but there was wood mixed in, too. The doors moved back and forth on an old pulley thing instead of opening in and out, and the windows were weird. They stuck out from the bottom like they were broken, but that's the way you opened them.

Horses were standing around outside stamping their feet, swishing their tails. I guess that's how they keep the bugs away. There were lots of flies and usually I can't stand that, but I wasn't feeling no irritation just then. Man, it was the horses. They were so big, big and shiny. You could see all their muscles and they weren't even flexing or nothing. I'd seen cops riding them during parades and stuff, but I never thought I'd be trying to ride one.

The barn was surrounded by fields closed off by gates, so you had to walk on these paths in between the fields to get around the whole place. And there were horses behind all the gates, eating hay, running around, or just nipping at each other.

Looked like the kids over on the side of the barn knew what they were doing. Riding horses like they were in the movies. Some of them were smacking a ball around with a long stick. Now that was something. They were hitting the ball all the way down on the ground while they were up on their horses. This one dude had on a black jersey with a number three real big on it. Looked like he was telling all the other kids what to do.

"This is it." Dre, the brother who drove us over, was smiling all over his face. I never saw nobody looking as happy as he did. He's straight-up corny. Dre was one of the people who'd come to the house talking about how much kids can learn from horses. Said animals can teach you things like responsibility and caring. Said taking care of horses is hard work, but you can learn a lot of stuff and, maybe, get motivated to think about going to college and all like that. Dre talked about polo the whole time he was driving us over. And even after we got there, he just kept going on about how it was such a beautiful sport. Said it used to be in the Olympics, but not anymore.

The smell was the first thing that got on my nerves. It was sickening sweet. Not really, really bad, but definitely not good.

I pulled my shirt up over my nose like that was gonna help. Foster took off his hoodie, wrapped it around the bottom of his face, and tied the arms in the back. He's so skinny, he looked like a string-bean bandit or something.

"Troy, man, this where we gonna be?" His voice was muffled under the hoodie.

I draped my arm over his shoulders. "This place has your name on it, son." Real quick, I undid his hoodie and tied his arms behind his back. I knotted it tight and pushed him toward the horses.

"Don't try it, man."

"Who's gonna stop me?" I've always been stronger than him and he knew it.

"My posse's saddling up now."

"It'll be sundown before they get here," I said, pushing as hard as I could.

Me and him were both laughing. I had him up to the fence, real close to this dark brown horse's butt. Foster's arms were tied up, but he dug in his heels.

"Hey, you two, cut it out." Dre frowned at us. "Don't mess with the horses like that."

"We're just taking a look," I said. I was busy trying to stick Foster's head between the fence rails when I saw the horse looking at me. "Dang, is this thing cross-eyed or what?" I jumped back 'cause the biggest eyeball in the world was looking at me. It had long eyelashes and there was only one.

"I don't know, man, I think the other eye is all the way over on the other side of its head." Foster backed away from the fence, too.

"That's not very smart." A girl's voice came from behind us. "You're in the horse's blind spot. You could get kicked."

I started to tell whoever it was to mind her own business, but when I turned around and looked at her, the wind was sucked right out of me.

"Oh. Newbies," she said, laughing. "You can always tell by the clothes on the nose."

Standing in front of us was the hottest honey on the planet. Big brown eyes. That horse didn't have nothing on her in the eyelash department. She could have gone toe-to-toe with the horse in the skin department, too. Chocolate brown and fine. She walked on by in her high rubber boots and left me and my boy standing there looking stupid.

"Did you see that?" said Foster as I untied him.

"We definitely need to check this out."

Nobody told us we couldn't, so we slid into the barn. First of all, there was no sunshine. We were in a long hall broken up into these little rooms with a string of lightbulbs running down the center. Stacks of hay were everywhere with all kinds of riding stuff hanging on hooks.

"It ain't exactly dark and lovely in here," I said.

"Quit worrying about the girl, man. We're checking out our new offices."

My boy was right, but I didn't like the smell. All the horses were outside, but that didn't mean there weren't animals up in there. I saw at least two dogs and a whole lot of cats laying around. Something swayed in the back of one of the stalls. Something with horns and, look like, a little goatee.

"Yo, man, what is that?" I asked.

"Looks like the new assistant principal, Mr. Paul."

"That's cold."

"But true."

Foster was right. Our school had problems. Mr. Paul was one of them. He'd throw you in detention for the least little thing.

We were checking the joint out when we heard something like thunder going by. Took me a minute to realize that was the sound of horses running around outside. Right on the other side of the wall.

Then Dre came trooping into the barn with the two other new kids and this tall dude. Brother had on white, look like, stretch pants tucked into these brown leather boots. Had pads on his knees and a jersey that I could tell cost a lot of money. To top it all off, he had brown leather gloves that matched his boots.

"I was wondering what happened to you," said Dre. "Oh, I see you've met our mascot, Percy."

"Now we know his name," I said, rubbing my chin, "but what is he?" I looked around at the other kids to see if they had my back.

"A goat." Dre's eyes narrowed. "What did you think?"

"I really didn't know."

He laughed. "Percy brings us good luck."

"Aren't we here to learn about horses?" this chunky dude asked. He looked like he really didn't want to be there.

"My question is, are we going to have to take care of this goat, too?" said Foster. "'Cause I'm going to need a raise if we are." We bumped fists on that one.

"Get over it." That's what he said. The tall dude. He said it without cracking a smile. Nobody knew what to say for a minute, but then Dre jumped back in.

"All right, everybody, listen up." He put his hands on his hips. "I'm Dre, as you already know." He took a little bow and we all clapped. "I'm the barn manager. I'm pretty much here all the time."

"That must be a drag on Saturday nights," said the chunky guy.

"Ready for house rules?"

The girl in our little group said no, but Dre went on anyway.

"Here we go. Number one, you check in with Winston, your program director, when you arrive and before you leave." He nodded at the tall dude. "We have to know where you are at all times. Two, you're here to work and take care of the horses. If you're good at that, then you can ride."

"Can't we ride first to see if we like it?" Foster asked.

Dre kept going. "No excuses, no exceptions. Three, beginners start by mucking out stalls." I didn't know what that was, but I didn't like the way it sounded.

"That's cleaning up after the horses and, as Winston just said, you clean up after Percy, too. Four, you go to school and don't start any trouble." He didn't say nothing about trouble finding us. That was more likely.

"What do you get for all this hard work?" he asked.

"We ain't getting paid, that much I know." Foster said what everybody was thinking.

"You can't put a price on what you're getting." Dre flashed a smile. "You get to ride. You'll get to learn as much about horses as you want. And if you're really good, you can play polo."

Foster raised his hand. Dre nodded at him. "Do you think I'll be playing polo before I get my driver's license?" All us kids cracked up. Dre, too.

"That all depends on you," he said. "Depends on how hard you work and if Winston thinks you're ready." Dre told it straight. "Some kids are riding right away; others never make it to the saddle. If you're interested in polo, you can try out next spring."

That seemed like a long time away, but none of us had ever been on a horse before.

"Okay," said Dre. "This is where I exit and leave you in Winston's hands."

I did a quick look around. Nobody wanted him to leave us with Winston. Dre wasn't bad. Winston was another story.

CHAPTER THREE

WE LIVE ON a block of row houses with big front porches. Some of the houses are messed up, like the boarded-up ones. They make everything look mean. There aren't that many trees to hide the bad-looking houses, either. When we were little, me and Foster used to jump the banisters and work our way down the street without ever touching the sidewalk.

The sidewalk's where stuff happens. Somebody got shot out there last summer. And there's always a bunch of guys hanging on the corner. Some of them are looking for work, some ain't no good, some just ran outta juice. The thing is, you gotta figure out which is which.

We were over Foster's house playing cards after that first day at the stables.

"So, what's on your mind?" Foster always asked me what I thought about stuff before I had a chance to ask him.

We were sitting on the floor, leaning against his bed.

Something about that day made me feel better. My chest felt open, like the thunder from the galloping horses stirred something up.

"The horses were sweet, but I don't like that dude Winston."

"Sweet, phew! Are we talking about the same place?" I knew what he was saying. Being the horse janitor wasn't going to be fun. This was May and it smelled bad already. "And did you see those polo dudes out in the field? They looked tougher than the football team over at Dunhill."

Foster picks up on everything. Pops says he's a perceptive young man, a good friend to have.

"Yeah, the polo thing," I said. "How come nobody ever heard of it?"

"Miss T said it used to be just for rich people." Miss T is Foster's mom. She's all right with me. She and Foster really helped me out when my mom passed. When I was upside down.

"Well," I said, "I don't know about you, but, like it or not, I have to stick with it." We both knew I might get expelled if I didn't. Foster skipped school sometimes, but not as much as me.

He put the cards down and looked at me with one eyebrow raised. "They beat people up over at Dunhill." Dunhill High School, where I'd end up. I didn't want Foster to keep talking about it.

I squeezed my eyes shut. "Smells like Miss T's getting busy downstairs," I said. The smell of her chicken gumbo made its way up to Foster's room. It was probably dinnertime at my house, too. "It's time to eat, man." I got up off the floor. "Check you out tomorrow." I picked up my backpack and headed downstairs. I stuck my head in their kitchen and waved to Miss T before I left.

The block was quiet. Most people were inside their houses. Everybody but Lay-Lay. He was leaning on a car across the street. We hadn't spoken since the iPhones thing went down. Best to just keep walking.

I KNEW POPS'S BROTHER, Uncle Ronnie, was over the house when I saw his motorcycle parked up on the sidewalk, right next to Mr. Glover's TV. Guess he figured Mr. Glover couldn't help but keep an eye on his bike while he watched his shows. Uncle Ronnie livened things up when he came over. He was on me soon as I walked in the living room.

"Hey, little man, you keeping busy?" He leaned forward in the reclining chair. "How the ladies treating you?"

"Not as good as you, Uncle Ronnie."

"I know that's right," he said, settling back. Uncle Ronnie had on his cowboy boots and leather hat. He was always worried about how he looked. Not like Pops. Pops could've looked better, but he didn't care.

"For God's sake, Ron. Will you give it a break? You been asking folks that for years." Pops been tired of Uncle Ronnie's ladies' man routine. Pops picked up the remote and turned off the TV.

"You know I taught you better than that. Real men respect women," a voice said.

Ooh, Grandmom. Uncle Ronnie busted big-time. Didn't nobody know she could hear everything from the other room. Grandmom came to live with us after my mom passed. Pops took that real hard. He still wasn't right from it.

"How much did you hear?" asked Uncle Ronnie.

"Enough," said Grandmom. She stepped from the kitchen doorway into the small dining room, where the table was set. "We can eat as soon as Ronnie takes his hat off." The skin on her face and neck was shiny with sweat.

Uncle Ronnie did what Grandmom said. "I ain't trying to disrespect nobody." He winked at me in the split second before his hat covered his face.

"Ain't?" said Grandmom, shaking her head. She put the fried fish on the table.

We all sat down and Pops changed the subject before Uncle Ronnie set Grandmom off again.

"So, how's things in the park?"

I made a quick calculation: Do I play it cool or tell it straight?

"All right," I said, going for cool.

"All right? Is that all you have to say?" Pops pointed at the coleslaw, asking Uncle Ronnie to pass it to him. "I wish I'd had the chance to work with horses when I was your age."

Grandmom reached over and patted my hand. "This is a good thing, Troy. We don't want you to end up like some of these other young men around here."

I wasn't in the mood for a lecture. I needed time to think about stuff on my own. I could like the horses, but I was scared of them. Didn't know what Winston was going to be like. Still wasn't sure what polo even was. It wasn't b-ball, wasn't football, wasn't boxing. Wasn't nothing I knew. Dre wasn't bad, but I didn't really want to be all horsey like him.

That girl was fly, though. Pops used to talk to me about girls. You know, how to act when you go over to a girl's house and how they want to be treated, but he didn't feel like talking much right now.

And the other animals were another thing, goats and all that. They were totally new to me. We never had a cat or nothing. Pops said they would have been just another mouth to feed. The only animals I knew were some bad dogs around the way that I did my best to stay away from.

Like I said, I was scared of the horses, but I wasn't telling nobody. Man, their flow was tight. They were beautiful, all power. Prancing around the yard, showing all their muscles and stuff. They looked like they would never be scared.

"I'm tired," I said, keeping my eyes down on my plate. "Had a hard day."

"A young man like you shouldn't get tired so easy," said Grandmom. "Shoot, you're tall for your age and getting broader every day. Seems like you could keep going."

"Reminds me of myself," said Uncle Ronnie, sprinkling hot sauce on his fish. He never missed the chance to relive his younger days through me. "I was handsome, too, and shot up real fast. I spent a couple of years tripping over myself. Troy's lucky, though—he's already got a slide that it took me a few more years to pick up."

Everybody always has something to say about my slide. I'm not bragging on myself; it's a fact. My mom used to say she couldn't say no to me when I turned on the charm. It's like a natural gift.

"Troy may look like you at thirteen but let's hope that's where the resemblance ends," said Pops. He never misses his cue to put Uncle Ronnie down. That's one thing that hadn't changed.

CHAPTER FOUR

MUCKING OUT. You need rubber boots to do it. That tells you all you need to know. At first, me and Foster hoped nobody on the block would see us in our boots. Mr. Glover was the one who called us out. He was always in front of his house, sweeping the sidewalk, watching TV, or directing traffic. He'd been around forever. It was hard to tell how old he was 'cause he was in real good shape. He stopped us one morning when we were getting on our bikes.

"You two look rather enterprising." Mr. Glover always talked like that.

"They're just rubber boots," I said. "Nothing special."

"Oh, but it's always special when a man changes his footwear." He couldn't just say shoes. It had to be footwear.

"Whatever. We're taking care of some horses."

"Figured something like that. The smell was a dead giveaway." It wasn't a put-down; he didn't look mean when he said it. Mr. Glover was right about the smell, though. It got all in your clothes, your hair, everything. Everybody who came anywhere near us would know we were around animals.

And Winston, who liked to dress, even he changed out of his leather boots when he showed us how to clean the stalls. He did that our second day at the stables.

"Don't try to muck out a stall when the horse is in it," he said to the group of us new kids. We were standing under the lightbulbs in the barn. He opened the door to a stall—that's what the little rooms are called—so we could see inside. The tops of the stalls were open to the barn's high ceiling. The stall doors were half doors, really. So when the horses were inside, they could still see what was happening in the barn.

"You'll have to maneuver around the animal. I don't recommend that. The first thing you have to do is assemble your tools so you won't find yourself standing with a shovelful of manure and nowhere to put it. Bring your pitchfork and shovel in the stall with you. Put your wheelbarrow close to the stall door. Troy, why don't you demonstrate while I walk you through it?"

"I can't really demonstrate since I don't know how to do it," I said, looking around at the other kids. That's when I saw her. The girl. She was standing back from our group. I watched her smooth her dark brown locs back from her face and tie them behind her head. Everything about her was delicate.

"We're all here to learn. There's nothing to be afraid of."
I knew he would do that. He set me up. I walked into the
stall. Winston, Foster, and the other kids were at the door.

"What you want to do is pick out the manure and
wet straw with the pitchfork and dump it in the wheelbarrow. Troy?"

I did like he said but the wheelbarrow was behind everybody, so I had to carry the pitchfork outside the stall. Poop
was dropping everywhere.

"Now, as you can see, this is not the way to do it," said
Winston. "The wheelbarrow should be in the stall so you
don't have to keep picking up the same stuff."

"It wouldn't be a problem if you weren't in the way,"
I said.

"This is a demonstration, Troy. No one's in the way.
We're observing."

Foster pushed the wheelbarrow through everybody. He
set it down in the stall. I tried to get all the crap up with the
pitchfork, but it kept falling through.

"Sometimes it's easier to pick up the wet straw with a
shovel."

"Why didn't you say that before?" I asked. I dropped
the pitchfork and used the shovel to fill the wheelbarrow up.

"We have one area behind the barn where we dump the
wheelbarrows," Winston said, pointing toward the back
doors. "Troy, can you take your wheelbarrow outside without

tipping it over?" He said that 'cause he knew what was going to happen. And it did. The wheelbarrow tipped over. I tried to straighten it up and my cell phone fell out of my pocket. Yeah, you got that right. It fell right on a turd.

Everybody lost it. The chunky dude was down on his knees almost crying. The new girl's shoulders were shaking so hard I thought she was getting happy. Foster didn't want me to see him laughing, but he was cracking up. It looked like he was kissing that goat, Percy, over in another stall.

"Two things could have been done to avoid this," said Winston, flicking dirt off his sleeve. "First, you should have the wheelbarrow face the direction you'll be going in. It's easier that way. Second, a full wheelbarrow tips over very easily. Never fill it all the way up."

Winston was messing with me. Testing me like everybody always does. Part of me was ready to walk out, but that's what he wanted me to do. I don't go down that easy.

"Guess I won't be texting tonight," I said, trying to shrug it off.

"You sure won't." It was the guy we saw in the polo field the day before. The one with the number three jersey. He looked like he was a little older than me and Foster.

"I think I heard your camera click," he said. "You'll have a photo to refer to later."

"We can do without the smart remarks, Jerome," said Winston. Jerome walked over to our group. Tried to act like he didn't care, but he was checking everybody out. He wasn't taller than me, but he was bigger all the way around. I knew his face, though. Just couldn't place it. "Jerome's been with us for, what is it now, three years?" said Winston.

Jerome corrected him. "Four."

"He's a good rider and an even better polo player." Winston was proud of him. You could see that. "You guys can learn a lot from him."

"Look me up anytime," said Jerome. "Best to text me"— he nodded at me and added—"if you can."

CHAPTER FIVE

GRANDMOM THINKS WANTING SOMETHING bad enough will help you get it. That ain't true. After my mom passed, I wanted Pops to keep everything together, but he didn't. I wanted him to keep talking to me about girls and things going on around the way, but he stopped. I didn't have much faith left in wanting or in anything good happening after I lost both of them—my mom to dying and my pops to being sad. When Pops wasn't looking beat down, he was just sorta snapping on everything like nothing was right anymore. And it was really bad at night when the house was quiet except for his pacing. I don't think he knew I could hear him, but he probably couldn't stop even if he did.

My mom always said I had a natural charm. She said she could just wrap herself up in it. Felt like that was all I had left. I mean, everybody's always saying you should use what you got. So that's what I did. Monday morning I was, you know, brand-new. For the past eight months, I'd been finding something else to do during the day. Walking in the woods, going to the movies, even hanging out in an old video arcade. That was my usual thing. But that Monday, I played it straight up. School was a part of the horse thing, so I had to act like I was into it. Wasn't hard 'cause nobody, not even the teachers, pretended our school was teaching anybody anything.

First-period math teacher, Mrs. Witherspoon, out sick. Substitute sat there and read the paper. Dude acted like he was home on a Sunday afternoon. Second period, history. Mr. Bell still showing movies. That's all he ever did. This one was about the Great Depression. Who needed a movie to see that? All we had to do was look out the window. Easy.

I needed to get my cell back, so I went straight home after school, changed into my boots and rode my bike over to the stables. I didn't expect that fly girl to be there, but she was. She was in the big, wide side doorway brushing one of the dark brown horses. Looked like she was talking to the horse, too.

"Hey," she said. I looked around to see if anybody else was there. Nobody. She was talking to me.

"Hey." I was glad I had on my rubber boots. At least I looked the part.

"I'm Alisha."

"Troy."

"I know," she said. I didn't ask how she knew. She was in

the barn when Winston and Jerome jammed me. I wasn't trying to remind her of that.

"I have something of yours," she said, pulling my cell out of her pocket and tossing it to me. "Don't worry, it's clean."

"Thanks."

She'd finished brushing the horse and was picking up its legs, looking at its hooves. "You're new to all this, huh?" She could tell I didn't know what to do with myself. "Want to touch him?" She stood back up. "He's nice and happy now."

The horse, Luke, couldn't run away 'cause there were long ropes on either side of him to keep him under control. I moved next to Alisha and felt the horse's side. The hair was soft like a rug, but I could feel how strong he was. Real solid. His hair was the same color as raisins, shiny like how the dining room table looks after it's polished. Luke shifted his weight on his hind legs and I jerked my hand away.

"He's just getting comfortable," she said, patting him on the shoulder. "Want to give him a carrot?" She pulled a big piece of carrot out of her pocket and handed it to me. "Just hold your hand out flat."

I put my hand up to the horse's mouth. He had a real big tongue. Then I felt these soft lips just breeze across my palm and take the carrot.

"See," she said, "nothing to it."

She unhooked the ropes from the leather thing the horse had on his head, the halter, and started to lead him down the long hallway back to his stall. I walked along with her, making sure I wasn't behind the horse. That big animal was so smooth; Luke wasn't clumsy or nothing. And Alisha, as small as she was, wasn't scared of him. Some of the other horses made sounds when we walked by their stalls. Like they were calling out to Luke. I was afraid he would step on a cat, but the cat moved out of the way at the last minute. All these animals just knew how to be with each other. We walked down to the stall with Luke's name on it and Alisha put him inside.

"Troy." It was Winston calling from the front of the barn. "Breaking the rules already?" He was washing the mud off a horse's legs in this big shower stall.

"He's with me, Uncle Winston," Alisha said.

"Wait a minute," I whispered. "That dude is your uncle?" I was looking for the family resemblance. Winston looked all right, but Alisha was beautiful.

"So I see," Winston called out again, "but what's rule number one?"

"Check in with you," I said, stepping out from behind Alisha. Didn't want her to get into trouble because of me. I walked down to Winston. "I just came to get my cell."

"Doesn't matter why you came." He finished getting mud off the horse and straightened up. "The fact is, you're here." I couldn't tell if he was mad because I was in the barn or mad because I was talking to his niece. "Horses can be dangerous," he said. "For instance, what would have happened if Luke had stepped on your foot?"

Stepped on my foot? Was this dude for real? I shrugged.

"My point exactly." He scraped excess water off the horse with this rubber thing. "Don't let it happen again." The horse he was cleaning off was sorta nibbling on him. He patted the horse's neck.

"Well, since I'm here," I said, "is there anything I can do?" He didn't expect that.

"So, you want to produce," he said, looking me up and down. "You can make Dre happy by sweeping the aisle." He pointed over to the far corner, where rakes, brooms, and brushes were hanging from the wall. At least it wasn't mucking stalls. He put his horse away and went out to check on the others that were still outside.

"Produce what?" I said when Alisha walked down to me.

"That's just his way of encouraging people. You know, some folks are lazy. He wants all the kids to work hard."

Pops used to encourage me, back when our family was still in one piece. I looked out at Winston again. He was rubbing a spotted horse's face and smiling.

"Don't take this the wrong way," I said, "but he's not crazy, is he?"

"No, but he's going to work you." Just what I needed, somebody else on my case. Alisha must have read my mind.

"Uncle Winston's tough but he would give the shirt off his back to help the kids around here."

How was this dude going to help me? I swallowed hard. Was he going to bring my mom back? Was he going to make Pops happy again?

"His shirts are nice," I said, "but it's the boots I'm after." We both laughed. "How long have you been around horses?"

"Practically all my life. Uncle Winston raised me with them. He took me in after my parents died."

My mom died, too . . . I wanted to blurt it out but I couldn't look lame like that.

CHAPTER SIX

EIGHT O'CLOCK SATURDAY MORNING me and Foster were back at the stables. That's when they start feeding the horses and cleaning the stalls. Winston wanted the barn to shine. That's what he said. How he expected cobwebs and dried grass to shine, I didn't really know. All I can say is it was hard work, real hard. Besides mucking out the stalls, there was lots of sweeping, carrying, dumping, nobody ever just sitting around.

After we cleaned the stalls, Winston brought us new kids around the horses. Real slow at first. Said he'd learned the hard way not to take it too fast. They never had an accident or nothing, but you could see how something could go wrong.

You should've seen all the different horses. Most of them were dark brown but some were almost black. They had some that were all white and a few were white with dark spots. And their faces were all different. Like some of the brown horses had a white patch on their foreheads or between their eyes.

Man, all of them, all of them, were built. They didn't have any fat horses. And as strong as they were, they were gentle. They weren't trying to hurt nobody.

This was only our second weekend at the stables but we were learning a lot of stuff already. Like you have to know what you're doing with horses 'cause they get scared real easy. Spooked. That's what it's called. That was news to me. I didn't think they'd be afraid of nothing. You have to be careful about how you walk up to them and where you stand around them, stuff like that.

Winston took us over to a little field—he called it a paddock—with just one horse. I knew it was Luke; I could tell from his raisin color and long black mane. Anyway, Winston wanted to show us how to move around a horse.

"You guys just watch," he said. He led Luke a little bit away from us and tied him to the fence with a special knot. "Horses weigh between eight hundred and twelve hundred pounds, so you don't want to upset them."

"They weigh that much and they don't eat meat?" I asked.

"Very good," said Winston, nodding at me. "They eat mostly grass and hay." Winston had a way of always looking sharp, like nothing could knock him off his game. He looked neat even standing there in the dirt. "It's very important that you be peaceful and calm around these animals."

We sat there on the top railing of the fence and watched Winston talk to Luke.

"This is so lame." The chunky dude leaned over me, whispering loud. His breath smelled bad. I put my hand up to stop him from getting all in my face.

"Never approach a horse from the front or the back," Winston was saying. "Instead approach him from the side so he can see you." He was standing at Luke's left shoulder, petting him. "Your voice is the second most important way to communicate with a horse. Your hands are number one. Use your hands to communicate with a horse first."

"I'm gonna communicate with my feet in a minute," the chunky dude said, crossing his arms over his chest and looking up at the sky. He nudged the new girl with his elbow. "I gots to get outta here, you know what I'm saying?"

I looked at Foster but he was watching Winston run his hands all over Luke. Winston started at his nose, then went around his ears, down his neck to his shoulders and body. Winston was moving alongside Luke in slow motion until he got to his backside.

"Now, pay attention," he said. "I'm going to show you how to get from one side of a horse to the other safely." He kept one hand on Luke's butt and stepped behind him to the other side. Luke's tail never stopped swishing and Winston talked the whole time, saying stuff like *I'm right here, Luke.* He worked his hands back up Luke's other side to his head and down to his lips. Very smooth. Looked like Winston and Luke were best friends, totally cool.

Winston untied Luke and brought him closer to where we were, to the water bucket hanging on the fence. Luke stuck his mouth in the water but we didn't hear slurping.

"Is he drinking?" I said. "How come we don't hear nothing?"

"Horses drink silently," said Winston. "They suck the water; they don't lap like dogs and cats."

"We make more noise than that when we drink," I said, grinning at Foster. The chunky dude and the girl rolled their eyes but I wanted to know how Luke could be so quiet.

"It's grace," said Winston. "You may not know what that word means now, but you will if you're around horses long enough."

Luke brought his head up out of the bucket, and water dribbled out of the side of his mouth.

"Oh, that's graceful," said the chunky dude, twisting his lips out real far. He and the girl laughed.

"Can I get closer to him?" I said.

"Sure." Winston nodded. "Just be mindful of what you learned."

"That's right." The chunky dude twisted around toward me, waving his arms. "Be very, very mindful . . ." he said, all loud.

"Man, why don't you just shut up?" I jumped down off the fence and landed hard. Luke jerked back from Winston and stretched his long neck around to see what was going on. I sorta froze, not knowing what he was gonna do.

Winston whispered to Luke and patted his long neck. Then he turned back to us. "That's exactly the kind of behavior that could get someone hurt." He squinted his eyes like he was trying to figure me out. "Since you have so much energy, I'll have to find some extra chores for you." He pointed at me and the chunky dude. "Both of you."

The chunky dude sucked his teeth but he didn't say nothing else. I was still frozen in place. Luke's ears were perked up but he was calm. I wanted to get next to him, so I tilted my head in his direction.

"All right, Troy," Winston said, "if you're settled down, Luke's still waiting for you." I took a deep breath and walked over to Luke's left side. I put my hand on him and moved it up over his shoulder. He shifted his weight a little bit, but I didn't jump like I did the other day in the barn with Alisha.

"Here, you hold the lead line," said Winston. He handed me the rope and stepped aside. Luke sniffed around my head and shoulders, then put his head in the bucket to drink some more water.

"Let him drink as much as he wants," said Winston. "He's comfortable with you." Right then, Winston didn't seem so weird and Luke didn't seem so strange. Everything was cool until, all of a sudden, I felt a spray of water all over the side of my face and shoulders.

"Is that close enough for you?" the new girl said, giggling behind her hand. The chunky dude was laughing along with her; Foster wasn't.

"Horses do that sometimes," said Winston. "They wash their mouths out just like we do."

I squeezed my eyes shut. I didn't like being laughed at. Seemed like everything I did at the stables just sorta backfired. But, I don't know, I didn't want to quit. I opened my eyes and saw Foster frowning, not at Winston or the chunky dude. He was frowning at me. Thinking about it now, he could probably tell that the horses were already drawing me in. You know, he probably thought he was losing me. I'd told him about Pops's pacing at night. Maybe he could tell that when I lay in bed listening to that, the only thing that made me feel better was the horses.

CHAPTER SEVEN

DRE RAN THINGS at the barn. The dude even lived there. In a little apartment upstairs. I don't think I would've wanted to be out in the middle of that big park, in the middle of this big city, in the middle of the night, but he did. All these old houses and big statues. I'd be afraid they would come alive or something.

Dre was always real busy but he stopped to talk to me and Foster when he saw us standing over by the field where they practice polo. We were watching two of the players, Willie and Little Keith, on their horses hitting a ball around.

"You see what they're doing, right?" Dre put the bucket of grain he was carrying down on the ground.

"Yeah, moving the ball down the field to try to make a goal," said Foster. "Look how they keep bumping into each other even while they're riding."

"Oh, if you like to get physical, try polo," said Dre.

I leaned against the railing. "We don't really know the game."

"I didn't know it before I started coming here, either." He pointed down to the ground with his two index fingers. "This place got me started. Then I played in college, too."

"You can play polo in college?" Foster asked.

"Depends on the school." Dre took off his baseball cap and wiped his forehead with the back of his hand. "Not everywhere."

"How come nobody ever heard of it?" I said. I really wanted to ask him how he came to be living with all these animals, but I didn't.

"It costs money, that's why. You gotta know how to ride and you have to have access to horses."

"Yeah, in hoops all you need is the ball," I said. "And the hoop."

"But I'm telling you, if you aren't afraid of getting rough, check it out." He did a fake dribble and pass. "It's like b-ball on horseback." He picked up his bucket of grain and headed back inside the barn.

"We're both good at hoops," I said to Foster.

"Yeah." He looked down at the ground. "But you're the one with the flow."

"Flowing through what?" Jerome had come up behind us. "Horse turds?"

He had a way of just popping up without you knowing it. He was carrying a shovel. He threw it so it landed at my feet before he walked off laughing.

"Doesn't he remind you of Lay-Lay?" Foster said.

"He does, same nose and forehead."

"But he's not from around our way." Foster sat on the railing's middle bar. He picked up the shovel and drew circles in the dirt with it. "He's from the suburbs."

"Who told you that?"

"He did."

"I don't care where he's from," I said. "Why can't he be cool?"

"Just stupid."

It was getting cloudy. I held out my hand and felt some raindrops. "It's starting to rain," I said, looking up at the sky. "We should see if they need us."

Foster drew a stick figure of an animal in the dirt and handed the shovel to me. Cracked him up to see me ride that thing like it was a horse.

I wanted to see how the horses would act in the rain since they didn't have umbrellas but it only rained a few drops before it cleared back up. We didn't have anything else to do, so me and Foster went to Winston's little office to tell him we were leaving. We weren't sneaking around or nothing but the door was open, so we could hear him talking to Jerome.

"Whoever we get is going to have to be good," Winston was saying. We heard a chair scrape against the floor like somebody was getting up.

"Yeah, it's too bad Marcus is moving away before the exhibition match." Jerome added, "He's almost as good as me."

"Well, the sooner we get another person on the team, the better."

Sounded like Winston turned off the computer just as Foster raised his hand to knock on the door. Jerome must have been standing right there 'cause he snatched the door open wide.

"We're leaving," Foster said.

"Don't get into any trouble on your way home." Jerome just had to say something.

"Okay," said Winston, "see you tomorrow at eight."

We nodded and turned around just as Dre came in the side door, leading this real spunky little horse. She was smaller than most of the others we'd seen. Winston got up from his desk and came out into the hallway to get a better look at her.

"How's she doing?" he asked. She was reddish brown with a mane the same color. The mane had been trimmed so it was real short. And the tail was braided like a girl's hair.

"You know Magic," Dre said, moving his hand over her shoulder. "Always ready to go."

This horse—I don't know how to say it—she moved like she did have someplace to go. You know, like she had her mind set on something.

"Magic's a polo pony," Winston said to me and Foster. "Highly spirited and—

"Kick-ass," said Jerome.

Winston cut his eyes at Jerome. "I wouldn't have used that word," he said, "but she's a horse that's been trained specifically for polo. "

They all looked at Magic like she was their little baby daughter. Felt like me and Foster were on the outside looking in. I wanted to be on the inside. I liked that little horse's fire.

CHAPTER EIGHT

YOU COULD TELL who was into the horses and who wasn't. All you had to do was look at Alisha and see the girl was happy. She was in the barn Sunday morning singing. She wasn't embarrassed about it, either. The other two new kids, the chunky dude and the girl, they definitely weren't down with it. They didn't come back on Sunday.

Winston didn't let me off the hook, though. He gave me extra work to do even though the other dude, the one who started the whole loud thing, was gone. Felt like Winston cooked up a special job just for me. He said he didn't want mosquitoes to get out of control so I had to go around the whole place filling in all the big holes with dirt so they wouldn't hold water when it rained. There were always flies and other bugs around, but Winston said we could do more to prevent things from getting worse. So there I was, pushing a wheelbarrow filled with dirt up and down the paths all around the place looking for mosquito hiding places. Winston said everybody would thank me later. Yeah, well, it felt like every time I filled in one hole, two more popped up.

I was taking a break, sitting down beside the wheelbarrow, when Foster caught up to me.

"Man," I said, "I'm never complaining about mucking out again." My T-shirt was drenched with sweat and, I swear, I was panting like a dog.

Foster handed me an orange soda. "Don't do any more," he said.

"I wish you'd said that two hours ago." I wiped my sweaty forehead with the back of my hand. "I'm almost finished now."

"You're never gonna finish, Troy. Jerome's got some kids making new holes."

I just sat there, looking at my boy. Foster looked away.

"You know, you sorta brought this on yourself." He kicked a stone around with his rubber boot.

"How do you figure that?"

"Asking all those questions yesterday," he said. "I mean, I'm glad that other dude is gone, but some of this stuff is stupid." He traced the outline of a horse in the air, imitating what Winston had done with Luke the day before. "That's dumb, man."

I took a long swig of soda. What Winston showed us yesterday wasn't dumb; I'd been thinking about it when I fell asleep last night. "You know my situation," I said.

"Yeah, well, your situation is everybody's making you look bad." Foster's chest was sorta caved in. "I don't think that was part of your plan," he said.

I heard a Mister Softee truck in the distance. Its tinny music sounded even more out of tune than usual. I squeezed my eyes shut.

"I had enough for today," he said. "I'm leaving early."

"What are you going to tell Winston?"

"Winston? Nothing." Foster had already started walking away. "I don't feel good," he said. "I'll find Dre and tell him I'm sick."

Everybody's making you look bad. That's what Foster said. He was right; that wasn't my plan. I finished the soda and watched Foster go off before I pushed the wheelbarrow back up to the barn. Alisha saw me coming and walked down to meet me.

"Where's Foster?" she said. "He's going to miss the polo match."

I walked right past her with the wheelbarrow. "What?" I said over my shoulder. I didn't stop pushing the wheelbarrow 'cause I wanted to get rid of it in the barn as quick as I could. "A polo match here?"

She had to walk fast to keep up with me. "Yeah, there's a team from Jersey here to play a pickup game with our guys."

I thought about trying to find Foster so he'd come back, but he'd probably just tell me I was lame. Maybe Dre'd tell him about the game. I pushed the wheelbarrow up the little ramp in front of the barn and took it inside.

I'm telling you, everything about the place was different. Man, that old barn was alive. And for the first time, I could see which horses had been trained for the game. Their tails were braided so they looked like they'd just come from a beauty salon. And they had bandages on their legs, too. Winston was in the middle of a bunch of guys and animals, directing everything. He was real serious about it, barking orders like a drill sergeant. And the whole polo team, Jerome, Willie, Little Keith, and Marcus, all of them, were dressed in white pants, jerseys, leather boots, and helmets.

I left the wheelbarrow up against the wall and went back outside. The Jersey team's horses were over by the polo field, all done up like ours.

"I thought you said this was just a pickup game," I said to Alisha. "A casual thing?"

"Nothing's casual when Uncle Winston's involved." She threw up her hands. "You should go over there and try to get a good spot. They're getting ready to start."

"What about you?" I said. "Aren't you going to watch?"

"I'm going to check on Uncle Winston first." She shook her head like this was something she always did. "He gets all wound up whenever they play." She looked a little worried when she disappeared into the barn.

I walked back down the path to the polo field. I could see guys riding their horses around, warming up. Man, they were good. Looked like the riders and their horses did everything in sync.

Our team came out with their horses led by Jerome and Magic; they were both profiling. I could tell from the way Winston was darting around that he was uptight. Pickup game or no, he wanted to win.

I couldn't really figure out what was going on. Horses and riders were everywhere before it settled down to just four players from each team and a couple of referees on the field. The players all put goggles on, so I figured the game was about to start. The next thing I knew, the two teams were fighting for the ball. And they weren't riding slow, either. They were going fast, but they could stop their horses on a dime and change direction. Looked like the players were running interference for each other, hitting the ball backward and forward, knocking into each other, stealing the ball from the other team, galloping and shouting. I heard somebody yell, "Turn it." Jerome reached out with his mallet and turned the ball around so he could take a better shot. He and Magic didn't miss a beat. How was he doing that? Then somebody called, "Tail it." Marcus stole the ball from the other team and smacked it back toward his horse's tail. Little Keith was right there to run it down the field.

They were yelling a whole bunch of other stuff that I couldn't hear and bumping into each other. Between the dust, and the shouting, and the flying ball, and the horses' thunder, I felt my heart beating real fast like it does after I run the fifty-yard dash.

I couldn't just go home after the match, so I went back over to the barn. Jerome and the rest of the team were taking care of their horses. Winston was in the middle of their little group talking real fast. They'd won but, from what I could hear, Winston wanted Little Keith and Marcus to work on their swings.

"Pretty cool, right?" said Alisha. She was standing at the bottom of the stairs that led to the second floor of the barn. "We're having hoagies up at Dre's," she said. "Come on up."

I hadn't been up in Dre's apartment before. It was above the front of the barn, over Winston's office and the horse shower stall. It wasn't as long as the whole barn but it was just as wide. He had a lot of open space up there that he had sectioned off into separate rooms. There was a kitchen with a wooden table and some chairs on one side of a bookshelf. On the other side of the shelves was his living room. He had a big rug with a red couch and a couple of old leather chairs sitting in front of a wide-screen TV. Up against the wall was a black exercise bench with weights scattered all around it. I liked these little Japanese lamps sitting on wooden crates sprinkled around the place. And there was another bookshelf hiding where he slept in the back. I wasn't surprised to see he had loads of animal books laying around the place. The funny thing about being up there was that the horses were right below. You could hear neighing and snorting no matter where you were.

"It must be spooky living up here," I said, standing at the top of the stairs. Alisha walked right over to the kitchen and plopped down at Dre's table.

"Spooky," said Dre. "What makes you think that?" He leaned a bulletin board he'd been sticking something on against the bookshelves.

"Well, you're all alone," I said, looking around.

"Are you deaf?" he laughed. "I'm not alone at all."

"He's got twenty horses living on his ground floor," said Alisha. "Besides, he's with us all day."

"Don't the horses keep you awake at night?" I asked.

Dre looked up to the ceiling like he could see the sky straight through the roof. "It's the total opposite," he said. "I sleep like a baby up here." Dre was smiling the way he does. His whole face was lit up like he was in heaven. We could hear the horses moving around in their stalls downstairs.

"So, Troy," said Alisha, "what did you think of the game?" She took a bag of paper cups down from the top of Dre's refrigerator and walked to the sink to fill one with water.

"Fierce." I grinned and shrugged. "That's about all I can say, man. You have to be fierce to play polo."

Dre laughed. "Could you follow what was going on?" He turned the bulletin board around so we could see it. *Star of the Week* was spelled out in big yellow letters across the top.

"Not really," I said. "It was hard to—"

"What's that?" interrupted Alisha. She finished drinking her water and pointed to the board.

"Oh," said Dre. "We're going to start, you know, acknowledging what folks are doing around the stables." He bent over and straightened up the big letter *S* that was drooping to the side. Alisha smiled at me and shook her head no while Dre was looking down. His idea was cornball, but we didn't tell him that.

"Here's what you need to know about polo," said Dre. "Matches are usually broken down into six periods. They're called chukkas and each one is seven minutes long. Each team has four players and they wear a number on their jersey that tells you what their position is." He'd fixed the *S* and sat down at his table. "Number one plays mostly offense, number four is predominately defense—defending his team's goal. Number two is also offensive but plays deeper. Number three is the most important player—basically, the quarterback." Dre looked real excited. "Number three has to be totally on point with hitting long distances as well as controlling the ball close in with his stick."

"That's what I had a hard time seeing," I said. "I couldn't tell what was going on when the horses were all bunched up together."

Dre nodded. "That's what makes Jerome so good. He's very good with his stick."

"The mallet, you mean? How long is that thing?"

"Yeah." The letter *S* on Dre's bulletin board had fallen back down. He bent over to fix it again. "How big is a mallet? That depends on a lot of things, like how big the player is and his hitting style." Dre scratched his head. "I guess the most common length is around fifty-two inches."

We heard Winston and everybody coming up the steps. "I think I smell food," said Alisha.

Jerome, Marcus, and Little Willie were talking about different hitting angles and all this other stuff, but Winston and Keith were carrying two six-foot-long hoagies.

"They can talk about polo forever," said Dre, "but take my advice, Troy. Grab something to eat quick because it won't be here long." He got up to get paper plates and napkins and, next thing I knew, the table was covered with meat, cheese, tomatoes, shredded lettuce, and bread.

"I'm glad you're here," said Winston, nudging me. "They looked pretty good out there, don't you think?"

He caught me with a mouthful of hoagie, so I just nodded.

"He's speechless," said Jerome, blowing up his cheeks like his mouth was stuffed with food. Little Keith and Willie laughed, and Jerome pointed to Dre's bulletin board. "But this . . . this Star board says it all. Who else would that be but me?"

CHAPTER NINE

FOSTER WASN'T IMPRESSED when I told him about Dre's apartment or the game. Said it sounded dangerous. I told him it was rough. Rough but beautiful. I tried to tell him how good those guys looked on their horses, how each player had his own style and beat and swag. I spent the whole week trying to tell him how we could look like that, too.

"I thought we were just doing this 'cause we had to," he said. "I'm not trying to be the next Winston."

How could he say that? Polo was dope, man. I couldn't stop talking about it.

"You should have seen Willie doing neck shots."

"He hit the ball across the front of the horse . . . under its neck?" Foster shook his head. "Now that I'd like to see."

"Well, you can, man. It can be you."

We always did everything together, so I thought he just needed a little more time to come around. I thought I had time to work on him slowly. I didn't know Winston was gonna kick everything up a notch that Saturday.

We'd finished cleaning the stalls and were outside with Winston and Luke. I remember how the sky was really blue, with streaky white clouds.

"Let's try some exercises so you won't be so afraid of the horses," said Winston.

I answered for me and Foster: "We're not."

"Not what?"

"Afraid of them."

"Oh, we're still playing that game?" Winston sighed real heavy like Pops does sometimes. "Look, you can't fool the horses. You have to be in tune with these animals or you could get hurt."

That shut me up.

"Luke's very gentle," Winston said. "He's taught a lot of kids how to ride."

"We're actually going to get up on him today?" Foster asked.

"Yes, bareback."

Me and Foster looked at each other.

"Without a saddle," said Winston. "I want you to see how it feels to be on a horse. Feel how he moves."

Up until then we'd been watching other kids ride. Now it was our turn. Winston went on.

"First, you're going to come closer to Luke, on his left side, and pat his neck. You're going to let him smell you, get used to you. Then you're going to get up on the mounting block and sit on him. When you're comfortable, you're going to lean forward and hug him with your arms around his neck. You'll sit back up and I'll use the lead to walk him around, just right here by the door and then, if you're up for it, you're going to lay back on his rump and let your hands hang free."

"With no hands?" I said.

"No hands."

"And why are we going to do all this?" Foster asked.

"You're building trust," Winston said. "Luke's very reliable. I want you to feel that."

I ain't going to lie; I'd been thinking about how cool I would look on a horse, but now I wasn't so sure.

"It sounds okay up to the laying-down part," I said.

"That's where the trust really comes in." It was Dre. He'd just come out of the office. "You decide how far you want to go," he said.

Now, I trusted my family and I trusted Foster and Miss T. I didn't know about trusting nothing or nobody else. Around my way, you had to keep your guard up. Here they wanted me to do the opposite. I looked at Luke, standing there waiting. I remembered how his lips felt on my palm and how Alisha led him around. I figured I'd been close to him before, and Winston and Dre were here. They wouldn't let anything bad happen, so I said okay. Winston looked at Foster and he nodded.

"Okay, you know where the tack room is, right?" Winston pointed to one of the rooms off the wide aisle inside the barn. "Go in and get a helmet. And pull your pants up, too," he added.

Me and Foster had been past this room but we'd never been in it before. There were saddles, halters, all this leather stuff on hooks on the walls. The whole room was just filled with it. Helmets were stacked on these big shelves on one side.

"It's going to be hard finding the right size for your big dome," I said, taking a helmet down. It was too small for Foster but I put it on his head anyway. I thought he'd knock it off but he didn't.

"That's all right," he said, searching the shelf for another helmet. "I'm wearing two for extra protection."

He was being funny, but not really. He didn't take that little helmet off until I told him I was going to get my cell and take his picture.

"We're stepping up in the world," I said as we walked back outside.

Dre was still there with Winston and Luke but he had another horse with him, too. It was that real pretty dark brown one me and Foster had seen on our first day. I checked her out real good. Her mane was black and it hung down over her eyes like bangs and she had white bands around her ankles that made it look like she had socks on. Her long tail was flicking back and forth.

"We have two of everything, so you can both do this at the same time," said Winston. I could see he really wanted us to try this. "Foster, you'll take Luke and, Troy, you're going to be working with Chance."

I walked over to Chance's left side and did what I'd seen everybody else do with the horses. I patted her on the neck. I still wasn't used to that big eyeball, but it didn't look so wack to me like before. I ran my hand over her shoulder and back.

"Don't be shy about talking to her," said Dre. "That way she'll get used to your voice."

"Hey, Chance, what's up?" That big eyeball took me all in. I didn't hear Foster talking to his horse, though.

Dre gave me the lead and, with him right beside me, I walked Chance over to the mounting block. There was another one for Foster.

Then we had a problem. Trapped by our pants.

"I can't get my leg up over this horse," said Foster. I didn't turn around to look at him 'cause I was afraid to take my eyes off of Chance. But I was stuck, too. My pants didn't give me enough room to swing my right leg up. Couldn't ease down onto the horse like Winston told us to. I was sorta squatting over Chance with one leg still on the block.

"I guess we're gonna have to start wearing pants like Winston," I said, trying to make a joke.

Foster picked up on it. "Miss T can't afford no stretch pants, even if I did want to wear them."

"Any time you're ready." Winston looked at Dre and shook his head. "I told you to pull up your pants, but you didn't want to listen. And these aren't stretch pants; this isn't the mall. Polo players wear breeches."

We heard Jerome and his crew laughing. They'd come around the side of the barn just in time to see us looking dumb. Chance was starting to paw the ground. Even she wanted me to get it together.

I hitched up my pants and swung my right leg over Chance, and I was on her back. I know I wasn't that far off the ground, but it felt like I was high up in the sky. I mean, I knew she was big, but it didn't really hit me how wide she was until I was sitting there. It was funny to look down on Winston and Dre from up there. Like I was on another planet and they were still down on Earth.

"Now, lean forward and give your horses a hug," Winston said.

I was afraid to touch her at first. Her neck looked so long I thought it might break or something, but she was real strong. Made me feel like a little kid again, hugging something like that.

"You ready to take a little walk?" Dre asked.

I didn't really want to stop hugging her, but I didn't want nobody to think something was wrong with me.

"Hold on to her mane," he said.

"It won't hurt?"

"No, it's not like our hair."

Chance took a few steps and I felt like I was riding an elephant. You know like you see in cartoons? Real lopsided, like you're going to fall at any minute. Dre stopped so I could straighten myself out. We started again and I could feel her shoulders moving her front legs. Her head was bobbing back and forth on her neck. I don't know why but I just started smiling. We went around in a little circle and stopped in front of the side barn door. Foster was there on Luke, too.

Winston looked at us real close like he was trying to see what we were thinking. "Now, if you want, you can let go of your horse's mane, put your hands behind you on the rump, and lay back."

Me and Foster looked at each other. "Okay," I said.

Dre was standing right there, holding Chance's lead, so I knew she wasn't going to take off or nothing, but it was scary to let everything go. I never do that.

I laid back and I could feel her backbone up against mine. Like we were connected or something. Next thing I knew, my eyes were closed and I could feel the sun beating down on me.

The sun was so warm it felt like I was laying out on a beach, but without the sand. And you know what came into my head? My mom. From out of nowhere. Laying there on Chance, I was seeing my mom. She was in the sunshine, all around me. Felt like how it used to be when she was still alive. I just let everything go. I wasn't thinking about fronting or nothing.

Nobody was saying a word. Then I heard Dre whisper, "I don't know who's more comfortable, him or the horse."

Winston's voice was soft, too. "There's some serious bonding going on here."

I could have stayed like that forever, but after a few more minutes, Winston said that was enough. I opened my eyes and everybody was looking at me. Foster was already sitting up and Winston had a funny look on his face.

"Okay," Winston said. "Sit back up, swing your right leg over, and dismount."

I slid back down to the ground and laid my head up against Chance's side. Didn't want anybody to know I had a lump in my throat, but it felt like Chance knew. She knew she'd made everything all right.

Winston didn't have anything else for us to do after that. I was glad 'cause, I don't know, I was sorta confused. The leaves on the trees looked greener and I noticed all the birds twittering around. Reminded me of how I'd felt in the wintertime when I was taking long walks in the woods all by myself.

I felt like that until me and Foster went inside the barn to get our backpacks. That's when I saw Jerome's drawings on Dre's Star of the Week board. One was of a cell phone sitting on a turd. But worse than that was the second one. He'd drawn a guy wearing baggy pants squatting over a horse with his eyes shut real tight.

CHAPTER TEN

CRYING. HOW'D WINSTON get me to almost crying up on that horse? That would've been totally uncool. At night, when my mom first passed, I couldn't help crying but I never did nothing like that outside the house. Never let my guard down. But that horse, Chance, being around her made me feel like I didn't have to hide nothing. I don't know, it's kinda hard to explain.

After that first ride, I told everybody how cool I was. I didn't need no saddle. I rode bareback and all like that. But I didn't say nothing, not even to Foster, about the other thing. So I was surprised when he brought it up. Not during the week. He waited until we were on our way back to the stables that next Saturday. We were on our bikes, cruising down that road that leads to the place. There wasn't any traffic, so we were riding right next to each other.

"So, Mr. Mellow, been dreaming about Chance all week?"

"Mr. Mellow," I said. "Where'd you get that?"

"You know that's your new name, don't you?"

"Since when?"

"Since you went into a trance." He threw his head back and crossed his eyes. "Oh, don't tell me you forgot."

The truth is, I'd been thinking about it all week. And looked like he'd been thinking about it, too.

"A trance?" I said. "Man, I was just catching up on my sleep."

"Yeah right." He flipped his hand at me.

"I caught a few z's," I said. "If you were smart, you would've done the same thing."

"Ain't no way I was going to close my eyes up on that big thing." He took his hands off the handlebars and spread them real wide. "You must really be into this," he said. "You go into a trance every time you come here."

That caught me off guard, so I stood straight up, sorta like a zombie. "Well," I said, "trance on this." I stayed like that for a few seconds, then took off on my bike. "Last one in looks like Percy the goat," I shouted over my shoulder.

We tore up that last stretch of road. I won.

THAT'S THE DAY Winston started giving us real horseback riding lessons. First, we mucked out the stalls; then he showed us how to groom the horses, you know, how to brush them and everything, before we rode. Not bareback, but with a saddle.

Riding was more work. The horses had to be taken care of before and after you rode. And you had to take care of the leather stuff, too. But even with all that, I liked being there. Sometimes it was hard to believe I was still in Philly.

Oh, and there was Alisha. She was in the tack room when I went in to put the saddle blanket I'd used back on the rack.

"It's starting to feel like you've been here forever," she said.

I looked around at all the equipment in the room. Just a little while ago, I didn't know what any of this was. "It's not bad."

"Not bad," she said. "Come on, you know you like it." She threw the cloth she'd been using to polish her horse's halter at me.

"I said it's all right." I bent down to pick up the cloth.

"Well, you know you passed his test."

"Whose test?"

"Uncle Winston's, dummy."

"He's just doing his job." I handed the cloth back to her.

"This is way more than his job," she said. "He doesn't waste his time on kids who aren't worth it."

"Worth it?" I frowned. "How do you know I'm worth it?"

"It shows," she said, looking straight at me. "You're not the same knucklehead you were when you started."

This time I didn't hide my face. "Knucklehead," I said. "I was never like that."

"You know what I mean," she said. "I was a mess for a long time after my parents died, too."

I squeezed my eyes shut. I'd never talked about this with anybody before. "Do you still miss them?" I asked.

"Yeah, but it gets better and . . . you . . . still have your dad, right?"

I took a deep breath. "Not really." I took another deep breath 'cause I felt my chin starting to tremble. "I don't really have my dad right now. He's sad all the time."

"Well, you're lucky you found this place," she said, leaning in to me. "This place makes everybody feel better." Her face seemed to shine right then. It was hard to believe she'd ever been sad. We didn't say anything else. There wasn't any need to.

Foster was waiting for me out in front of the stables. It was my turn to let Winston know we were leaving. He was in his office when I knocked on the door.

"Me and Foster are taking off," I said.

He waved me inside. Winston never beat around the bush. He just jumped right into whatever he had to say. "Have you ever been in a relationship?"

I'd just finished talking to Alisha, so I thought he was heading someplace I didn't want to go. "What kind of relationship?"

"I'm not talking about my niece, although I see you're friends." He leaned back in his chair.

"Well, if you hadn't jammed me on my second day, she may not have paid any attention to me."

Winston smiled. "I needed to see what you're made of," he said. "You been looking for something, right? You've done some stupid stuff but you're not a bad kid."

"What's it to you?" I said, looking out the window.

"You move well and you try to play cool, but if you're going to play with me and my horses, you need more than that."

I still didn't know where the conversation was going.

"You need heart," he said. "I asked you about relation-ships because I'm hooking you up with Chance. She's a polo pony and I think she's right for you."

"You make it sound like Chance is gonna be my girlfriend."

"She better be."

CHAPTER ELEVEN

I DIDN'T WANT TO BE the kind of dude who's scared of his girlfriend, but Chance was bigger than me, way bigger. She could jack me up if I didn't know what I was doing. So, soon as I got home, I started working out. I liked to use the front porch for stuff like that.

I pushed the red-and-white metal chairs all the way back up against the house so I had enough room. I was on my twentieth push-up when Mr. Glover had something to say. He was hosing down the sidewalk in front of our house.

"A bond exists between humans and animals." He'd rolled his army fatigues up above his ankles and he was wearing a pair of green flip-flops.

"I know."

"Are you establishing a rapport?"

"Mm-hmm." I was on my twenty-third push-up.

"Take your time with the courtship." He guided some

cigarette butts off the sidewalk with a stream of water. "It'll make for a much happier marriage."

"I'm not trying to have no horse babies. Just learning how to ride."

"Take the time to appreciate the animal," he said, all serious. "You won't regret it." I wondered how he knew so much about horses. He must have figured that's what I was thinking. "I'm not a horseman myself, but I grew up on a farm," he said, turning off the water. "Things always went better when you worked with the animals, not against them."

Mr. Glover rolled up his hose and took it inside his house. I stayed out on the porch and did fifty push-ups total.

There was something to what Mr. Glover said. I don't wanna get all mushy, but Chance was always on my mind. More than some girls I used to like. And it wasn't just one way. She was checking me out, too. Same with that goat, Percy. He was always watching everything. Like he had to make sure you were okay before he got close to you.

I stood up and started to rearrange the porch furniture when I felt somebody looking at me from the sidewalk. It was Lay-Lay. He had this little smirk on his face. His mouth was all red from this cherry water ice he was eating. He didn't try to wipe his lips or nothing.

"Long time no see," he said. He leaned up against Mr. Glover's car like it was his.

"Been busy."

"So I hear." He finished his water ice and dropped the crumpled paper cup on the sidewalk. "So, what, you're too good for the block now?"

"Who's saying that?"

"I just heard it somewhere."

"You believe everything you hear?"

Lay-Lay shrugged. "I'm just telling you what I heard."

The screen door opened behind me but I didn't turn around to see who it was. Didn't want Lay-Lay to think I couldn't stare him down.

"Nobody at this address cares about what you heard, Lay-Lay." Grandmom came out on the porch with her watering jar. She fussed over her plants before she looked back up. "Who threw that trash on the sidewalk?" she said. "Lay-Lay, please pick that up."

He kicked the crumpled cup off the sidewalk into the gutter. "What do I look like—a garbage can?" He crossed the street and headed down to the corner where a bunch of guys were hanging out. That dude must not have had nothing else to do 'cause he was still on the corner when I turned the porch light off before I went to bed.

CHAPTER TWELVE

ALISHA WAS TIGHT with all the animals, so at first, I thought it was a female thing. I wasn't sure if a dude could really be like that. Winston set me straight.

"Chance already knows you from the time you've spent grooming her," he said. "We're going to build on that." He always smiled at the horses and said thank you when they did what he asked them to do. "Watch how Chance is with the other horses, talk to her, play with her. Basically, act like a horse."

"Act like a horse?" I said. "I'm not getting down on my hands and knees."

"That's not what I'm saying. I want Chance to see you as a member of the herd. If she trusts you on the ground, she'll follow your commands more easily when you're riding."

Foster worked mostly with Luke. It didn't look like they had a thing like me and Chance did. Winston gave him the same advice, but Foster wouldn't do it. Said it was stupid. But if you asked me, it looked like Foster was scared of Luke. He was sorta jerky around him and never really wanted to be alone with him.

Me? I felt good with Chance. So I started acting like a horse. I stretched my back legs like she did. Shook my head like she did, too. Winston said I was a natural. I don't know about that, but what really got me was when Chance hugged me. She bent her neck over my shoulder and put her face against my back. Didn't nobody tell me horses got cute like that.

Being with Chance had me thinking about all kinds of stuff. Like what you could do if you could ride a horse. I didn't want to be no cop, but some of them got to be around horses all the time. That's what I wanted.

Grandmom said I was too big to be a jockey. She knew 'cause she went to the Kentucky Derby one year. That was a long time ago, before she had Pops and Uncle Ronnie. Said once you got into horses, you couldn't get them out of your blood. Said that's what was happening to me.

School didn't even bug me so much. I mean, Mr. Paul was still stupid and you could get in trouble for the least little thing but, mostly, I didn't let none of that bother me. Even when Mr. Bell told me I was wasting my time dreaming about horses.

"No way that's going to lead anywhere," he said. "Better stick to what you know."

Like I said, stupid. I just did what I had to do to get over to the stables.

I had Chance coming to me, following me, and she would stop when I said "whoa." Foster said I was like some dudes with their dogs. I wish. I could see Grandmom's face if I tried to bring Chance home. I would just bring her right up to the sidewalk. Yup, tie her up to the street sign right next to Mr. Glover's TV.

WINSTON HAD US RIDING every day we were at the stables. We always had to do our work first, but there was plenty of time left over to ride. I even talked Pops into coming over to watch. That was something. I couldn't even sleep the night before and that's unusual for me. I can sleep through anything, sirens, barking dogs, whatever. I spent the whole night going over everything, you know, how to get the horse ready for riding, how to mount, how to sit, just everything.

Pops hadn't been to the stables since we first started. Me and Foster were tacking up when I saw him standing there. He looked little compared to the horses. He had on his lucky jacket, though, his red Windbreaker. It made him look happy even if he wasn't.

"I see why you need the rubber boots," he said. "You're not scared of these big things?" he added, looking around at the horses.

"Nah." I was glad I didn't have to lie about that anymore.

"Hey, Mr. Butler," Foster said, lifting his chin toward Pops.

"Foster, I hardly see you on the block anymore."

"They keep us busy here."

"So I see," said Pops, turning to look at Alisha as she walked by.

We had saddles on the horses and were tightening the girths. Pops didn't say anything about the smell. Stuff like that didn't bother him. He walked all around the stables, studying everything. Then he sat down on the grass under a big tree.

I squeezed Chance with my legs and we started walking. Then, from out of nowhere, I had that feeling again that my mom was with me. I don't know, maybe Pops brought that feeling with him. We went round and round the yard and it felt like, somehow, our family was together again.

"If you're comfortable, cue her for a trot," said Winston, walking around the inside of the yard.

I looked over at Foster. His eyes were so wide, like they were ready to pop out of his head. "I hope I don't fall off this thing," he said. Funny, him calling Luke a thing.

"Don't tense up," said Winston. "You know what you need to do. Give the horse more rein so you get in the right seat."

Me and Chance didn't have any problems. We just flowed right into a trot, that's all.

Pops was standing by the fence in his lucky jacket. He looked lighter or something. Like a weight was coming off his shoulders. Foster stopped way before I did. Said his legs hurt from all the bumping up and down. Winston slapped him on the back, and Foster took Luke around to the back to hose him down. I just kept riding Chance around the ring.

"Way to go, Troy." Winston gave me a thumbs-up. Me and Chance slid back into walking before we went over to Winston, and I dismounted.

"You were great," Winston said, giving me a high five. "Keep this up and you'll be taking Marcus's spot at exhibition. You know his family's moving away."

Me, playing polo? "I thought I had to wait another year for that," I said.

"Not if you're really good." Winston looked over at Pops. "Polo is really about being a good horseman."

Me charging down a field on a horse? Winston blew me away.

I gave Chance a little sip of water before I took her around to clean her up. Man, me and her were riding strong. Pops came around to the hose before he left. He gave me a playful punch on the shoulder.

"My son riding a horse," he said, smiling. "I'll have to bring Grandmom so she can see you." I hadn't seen him smile like that in a long time. It made him look young again.

Dre was waiting for me when I brought Chance back around to the front of the barn.

"Whoa, little brother, what's this? A victory lap?" He slapped me five. "I've never seen a new rider progress like you."

That was one of the best days I ever had. I didn't know it was going to be one of my last good days for a long while.

CHAPTER THIRTEEN

THE NEXT SATURDAY, we went out to Blanchard Polo Club. It wasn't in Philly. It was about an hour outside the city, in the country. We used to go on family trips to the other side of Pennsylvania, but we never stopped in any towns along the way. Grandmom said it wasn't too long ago when we weren't welcome out there. She still wasn't sure about it.

Dre said Winston knew everybody in the polo world. Sounded like he was a big deal to these folks. He always dressed nice, but that day he could have been on the cover of *GQ*. The crease in his pants looked like it could cut you, and his white shirt set off his dark skin real nice. And his watch— what's that word they use to sell expensive stuff? *Classic*. It was shaped like a rectangle, in a socket so he could turn the face inside out with his thumb. When the face was down, you couldn't tell what time it was 'cause all you saw was a metal case. He said watches like that were first made back in the day to prevent polo balls from smashing the face.

Alisha was the bomb. Girl had on a white dress with a mean pair of leather riding boots. The shine on them almost blinded me. To top it off, she had on a straw hat with flowers on the brim.

Me and Foster had been dying to get a ride in Winston's two-seater convertible but Winston borrowed Dre's white van for the day. There wasn't much room with all the equipment Dre always carried around and Jerome, who invited himself at the last minute. Winston wasn't too happy about that, either. He'd had it out with Jerome about his drawings on the bulletin board.

We saw some funny stuff on the way to Blanchard. Folks dressed like the olden days. Saw a bunch of men with long beards driving these horse-and-buggy things. Winston said they were Amish.

"I'm starting to get sickside." That was Foster. He was all slumped down in his seat.

"Seasick. We're nowhere near water." Alisha turned around to look at him.

"I know, but all these little hills twisting and turning is getting to me."

"Most people think these rolling hills are beautiful," said Winston, checking out Foster in the rearview mirror. "You're the first person I've met who finds it sickening."

"Maybe you need to eat," I said.

"Don't worry about eating," said Alisha. "Wait until you

see the spread at the club." She turned back around, smiling to herself.

"Why do you think I'm here?" asked Jerome. Actually, nobody knew why he came with us. This was supposed to be a chance for me and Foster to see a pro match.

Alisha rolled her window down so Foster could get more air. "We've been invited into the VIP tent, thanks to Uncle Winston."

"We knew you were the man," Jerome said, tapping Winston on the shoulder.

I'd already seen our team play the Jersey guys, so I knew the basics. The game looked like it was just about getting the ball through the goalposts, but it was really about controlling your horse.

"It'll do you guys good to be on the scene," Winston said. We were pulling off the road onto this real long driveway. We weren't even at the club, but it was already beautiful. I never saw grass so green. And all the trees looked like they came straight out of a book, no vines or brown spots on them. The birds were even better than the ones we saw around our way, pretty red and yellow ones. Pigeons must not have been allowed out there. The driveway took us past fields with lots of horses. Everything about them was perfect.

"Who lives there?" I asked, pointing to trailers parked off to the side.

"Oh, those belong to the polo players," Winston said. "A lot of these guys travel around the country, playing on the circuit."

Finally, we pulled up near the playing field. There were bleachers on one side with some cars parked real close by. People were tailgating in little groups.

"Why didn't we bring any food?" Foster asked. "I'm starving."

Winston pointed across the field to a big white tent. "You're in for a treat," he said.

Just checking out the cars was already a treat. Winston parked the van between a Mercedes and a Jag and we walked over the polo field to the tent. All I can say is, he wasn't lying about the grub. We had shrimp, steak, the sweetest corn on the cob I ever tasted, ice cream, everything. And all the stuff they talk about on Grandmom's cooking shows was laid out, too. Oysters and all these cheeses that smelled kinda bad. The whole setup was like a wedding you see on TV. Tables with white tablecloths and flowers. Looked like there was a bar in every corner.

Winston was shaking hands with just about everybody. He introduced us to people who slapped us on the back and said they couldn't wait to see us on the field.

"So, you're part of Winston's hotshot polo team," this one old guy said. He was dressed funny, wearing faded red shorts with a yellow shirt and a green plaid jacket. "You must be good if you're with him."

Me and Foster weren't sure what to say, but Jerome loved all that kind of talk. "Just wait till you see us at exhibition," he said.

Looked like a lot of folks were just there for the party. Some guys in the tent were already drunk and it was only two o'clock. Some of the ladies, too. I saw why Alisha got dressed for this. Ladies were putting on a fashion show, trying to get everybody's attention.

Winston walked over to the edge of the tent so he could check out the players when they rode onto the field. They looked as good as their horses. Reminded me of how Winston looked the first day we saw him. They were flexing so everybody could see their stuff. Yeah, they were cool.

Me, I couldn't take my eyes off the horses. Problem was, I didn't know where to look. Horses were everywhere. On the polo field, running along the sides and standing at both ends. And there was that sound of thunder everywhere. It felt dangerous to be standing in the middle of all that.

Winston waved me and Foster over to sit with him when the match started. We had the best seats in the place, right on the center line. The umpire threw the ball in and the players went for it. It was like the tip-off in basketball but on horseback. The horses knew what they were supposed to do. They were bumping up against each other trying to get close to the ball. The players were bumping up against each other, too. They needed the pads, the boots, the helmets, all of it for protection. Nobody was holding back. One player got the ball and smashed it down the field. He took off after it and the other players lit out after him.

"Pretty exciting, isn't it?" Winston said. He was looking down the field through a pair of binoculars.

A player was hanging off the side of his horse, holding his mallet like somebody having a real good time at a house party.

"They let us sit so close to the field?" Foster asked. "We could be in trouble if one of these horses got out of control."

"They're ponies," said Winston. "Never horses."

"Whatever," said Foster, frowning at me. "They could hurt you."

"Only losers worry about getting hurt," said Jerome. "These guys know their stuff." He had worked his way over to where we were sitting.

"You're right to worry, Foster. This is a tough game," said Winston. "The ponies can go up to thirty-five miles per hour."

"That's what I mean," said Foster. "I should have brought my football helmet."

"Football," laughed Jerome. "Boy, where you from?"

"Well, unlike football," Winston said, cutting his eyes at Jerome, "there aren't any set plays. The players have strategies but they have to listen and keep looking behind to figure out where the next play will be since they're not facing the ball."

"Is that why they're all shouting?" I asked.

"Mm-hmm. They're at a gallop and they have to get their pony in line with the ball so they can pass it to a teammate or try to make the goal."

"Look at how the ponies are sweating," I said. "They're really working."

"Yes, they are," said Winston. "It's hot and they're going all out. In professional games, the players change ponies after each chukka. There's no way one animal could last the whole hour and a half."

I didn't know if I could last the whole hour and a half. Felt like I was high or something. I knew Winston and them were there 'cause I heard their voices but the sound of the mallets smacking the ball was louder.

"Earth to Troy." Alisha was nudging me. I hadn't even heard her walk over.

"What's up?" I asked, not taking my eyes off the field. That was deep. I never thought I'd pass up a chance to look at her.

CHAPTER FOURTEEN

WHEN I GOT HOME, Uncle Ronnie was over. He was down in the basement, whistling. Then I heard him staggering up the stairs with Pops's bike.

"I think I'll start cycling again," he said when he got up to the kitchen. "Might train for a bike trip down to Atlantic City."

Grandmom was watering her plants on the windowsill above the sink. Pops was sitting in one of the chairs at the little table looking out the window.

"It's safer than that motorcycle," said Grandmom. "As long as you're not going down there to gamble." She was always worried about stuff like that.

"Now you know I quit gambling." Uncle Ronnie rolled his eyes up to the ceiling.

"I hope so," she said, putting her watering jar away. "Always going down there losing money."

"You should get back into biking," Uncle Ronnie said, nudging Pops.

"I just might," he said, turning to look at us. I hadn't heard him pacing at night in a while. Maybe he was getting better.

"Well, if everybody's going to be athletic in this house," said Grandmom, "I may need to do something, too."

"Like what?" We all said it at the same time.

"I think there are some aerobics tapes still around here." She was peeking into cabinets like she expected those old tapes to be in with the cornflakes.

"We don't have a VCR anymore," said Pops. "Streaming is the thing now."

"Whatever," said Grandmom, waving her hand as she headed into the dining room.

That cracked everybody up. We hadn't done that in a long time. I held the back door open for Uncle Ronnie, and Pops went outside, too. The backyard was more concrete than grass but we used to have fun out there. A narrow alley separated the backyards on our block from those around the corner.

"You meeting a lot of new kids in the park, huh?" Pops said, watching Uncle Ronnie check the bike's tires.

"Yeah. Everybody's cool," I said, sitting down on the back steps.

"And what's that girl's name? The real cute one."

"There's a bunch of girls who ride," I said. "And girls can play polo, too."

"Really? Well, there was one there the day I came over. Looked like she knew her stuff."

"Alisha. She's Winston's niece."

"You talking to her?" That was his way of asking me if anything was happening.

"We're friends," I said.

"Is Foster friends with her, too?"

"Pops, there's nothing going on." He sounded like his old self but I didn't want to keep talking about this. The truth was, I really liked Alisha. A lot.

"I'm going over to Foster's," I said, reaching for the small polo mallet I'd left in the backyard. I wasn't hanging around for any more questions.

"Be back before ten," he said.

I WAS STILL HIGH from the trip out to Blanchard. Couldn't figure out how the players handled the horses and mallets without hitting the wrong thing. Looked like they could easily smack themselves upside the head. I had Foster looking for polo videos on YouTube.

"One hundred ten miles per hour," I said. "That's how fast the ball goes sometimes."

"How would that feel if it hit you in the face?" Foster's

eyes were fastened on the computer screen. We heard a police siren wailing a few blocks away.

"I'm wondering what happens if your horse gets hit," I said. "And what happens if you go down."

"Speaking of going down, did you hear Lay-Lay got in trouble?"

"What happened?"

"Man, you need to keep up with what's going on around here. He was running around Center City after the curfew they got down there. Now his mom gotta pay a three-hundred-dollar fine."

"Sounds like something he would do," I said.

"And," Foster continued, "know why we thought we knew Jerome when we first met him?" I shrugged. Jerome got on my nerves. I didn't want to think about him if I didn't have to. "'Cause he used to live around here." Foster should've been a detective. He was always snooping stuff out.

"Thought he told you he lived in the suburbs?" I said.

"He lives in the suburbs now, with his aunt." Foster turned from the computer to face me. "Remember that family around the corner? You know, the cops were always at their house?"

I remembered seeing cop cars at that house all the time. Grandmom said they did the best they could but the two oldest kids were on drugs pretty bad. They broke into a couple houses on the block before they got locked up. Turns out that family was related to Lay-Lay.

"Who told you all this?" I asked.

"Miss T," said Foster. "She was asking me about the kids at the stables. She remembered that one of Lay-Lay's cousins got into riding after his parents split up."

Foster nodded and pursed his lips when he saw my surprise.

"Yup," he said. "Jerome and Lay-Lay are cousins."

"So, Jerome is trying to act like he's not from around here."

I picked up the mallet and twirled it around, thinking about what Foster told me. I didn't know why Jerome had to act like he was something other than what he was.

Foster clicked out of YouTube. "I'm tired of watching this," he said, putting on some music to block out the sirens.

"I never get tired of it," I said, sprawling on Foster's beanbag. I held the mallet with both hands stretched above my head. "I wonder when Winston will take us back out to Blanchard."

"I'm not really worried about it," said Foster.

"What's not to like?" I asked.

"Being the only one," he said. "Felt like I was under a microscope."

I knew what he was talking about. The people at Blanchard were friendly, but it was weird to be someplace where there weren't many other black people. And it wasn't just that. Looked like everybody there had more money than we did, a lot more. The cars, the clothes, the horses. Everything like that.

"What about Winston?" I asked. "He's a brother."

"He's okay, sometimes, but then he starts putting on airs . . ." Foster's words trailed off. Winston could be proper but he wasn't putting on airs. That was just the way he was.

The windows in Foster's room were open. We heard a rustling sound like somebody was running up the alley. Couldn't be sure because the parachute covered most of the window and we had music on.

"The dude's wrapped too tight. Always correcting what you say. Like polo players don't wear stretch pants." Foster was doing a pretty good imitation of Winston, flicking dirt off his sleeve and checking his wrist like he was wearing a watch. I couldn't help but laugh. Foster kept going. "'This isn't the mall.' What's that mean? Ain't nothing wrong with the mall."

I felt the same way sometimes. Winston and Alisha were different from us. They didn't have to worry about money and they were always doing stuff we'd never heard of. And

Jerome, he was always trying to crack on us even though he was from our block.

"Jerome needs to get his butt kicked." Foster was on a roll now. "What's he got against football?"

"Probably can't play," I said.

"He better stay up on that horse, uh, I forgot, pony . . . never horse." Foster opened his closet and took his basketball out. "Riding's okay, but I miss shooting hoops," he said. He started dribbling across his room. It only took thirty seconds before Miss T shouted up the steps.

"Don't bounce that ball in the house."

Foster sucked his teeth, but he put the ball down on his bed.

"We can still play," I said.

"You gotta show on the block if you still wanna play. You can't just roll up on the court after you been missing in action." He was right about that. We spent no time on the block anymore. Then he said what I didn't want to hear. "I don't care if I never go back out to Blanchard."

I sat up and cradled the mallet in my lap. I couldn't wait to get back out to Blanchard. I wanted to be with Chance and make the polo team and all that. I'd hoped Foster would do it with me.

"You're not quitting, are you?"

Foster shrugged. He wasn't looking at me when he did

that, either. Normally, he was straight up about everything. He was acting different now.

"I'm not really into the horses like you are," he said. "Everybody knows that. Winston, Dre, Jerome." He gave a short little laugh. "Even the horses can see it. They don't take to me like they do to you."

"You and Luke could be tight if you wanted . . ."

"Not like you and Chance," he said. "Plus, I hate Blanchard. Too phony. Miss T said I don't have to go back out there if I don't want to."

"But you didn't see the polo match at the stables," I said. "That wasn't like Blanchard at all."

Foster shook his head. "Miss T is talking to Winston about what else I can do this summer. I may have to do some community service or something."

"I can't believe you, man." I frowned. "Community service . . ."

"Anything's better than polo," he said.

I squeezed my eyes shut. "So . . . humph." Foster's room had always felt like my second home but, just then, it felt like someplace I'd never been before.

"Troy, time for you to be heading home," Miss T called from downstairs.

It was almost ten o'clock. It only took a few minutes to walk from one house to the other, but Miss T always used her binoculars to watch the street when one of us was out after dark.

"Check you later," I said, picking up my backpack and the mallet. I tried to act like everything was cool even though my stomach was turning over on itself.

Outside was a little bit cooler than Foster's room, but not much. Our street was usually filled with kids on hot nights like this, but everybody was over at the schoolyard watching a basketball game. Mosquitoes were the only things hanging out. I was in front of Mr. Glover's house when a cop car spun around the corner. It sped up to me, stopped, and two cops jumped out.

"What's your name?" one asked.

"Troy Butler."

"What are you doing out here?"

"I live right there," I said, pointing at my house with the mallet. It was about the length of my arm.

"Drop it and put your hands up," he shouted. The other cop drew his gun. The first cop was on me before I could even blink, slamming me onto the hood of the car, twisting my arm hard behind my back, forcing me spread-eagle. He was breathing hard down my neck, running his free hand down my sides and legs. There was a sharp pain in my left elbow, but the cop was all over me, I couldn't straighten it out. The right side of my face was hot, pressed up against the car hood. I had to pee and I knew I couldn't hold it. I was dizzy and couldn't see straight. A buzzing mosquito was the last thing I heard before I passed out.

LIGHTS WERE FLASHING when I came to, flashing so, so bright. Pops was like a . . . a madman. His face was all bent out of shape—screaming, howling. Uncle Ronnie held him back with his body. "Dave," he kept saying. "Dave, Dave, he's okay."

I heard Miss T's voice: "I saw the whole thing." She held her binoculars up over her head. "This is totally unjustified. He spent the evening with me and my son."

Grandmom stood on the curb, next to Mr. Glover's TV, just looking down at her hands. She'd grasped his old antenna so hard it broke off in her hand. Foster took it away from her. A crowd surrounded us, chanting. "You're wrong, you're wrong, you're wrong . . ."

Was this my street? My street? Couldn't walk down my own street? Cops looking for kids. Grab me. Come grabbing me?

Mr. Glover worked his way through the crowd. His eyes were on fire but he calmed folks down. "Everybody, stay cool," he said. "We're here to support the Butlers. Just stay cool."

The wetness in my pants had traveled down my right leg to my sock. I crossed my arms over my chest and acted like I was looking around for my backpack. If I had it, I could hide.

If I had it, I could stick my head in it so nobody would see my face. I squeezed my eyes shut but I couldn't block out the clammy feeling on my right leg and sock.

Seemed like forever before I felt Pops's hand on my shoulder. "Here's your backpack." He handled it to me and pulled me into him real tight. Over his shoulder, I could see Miss T still holding her binoculars high in the air.

CHAPTER FIFTEEN

NOBODY WAS ARRESTED. Well, nobody should've been. Ain't nobody do nothing wrong. Cop said he felt threatened. They were looking for somebody who committed an armed robbery. Armed with what? A stick? And what'd the guy look like? Did he even look anything like me?

The cops called an ambulance, called for backup, too. I just wanted to get out of the street, but I had to be checked out because of what happened. Cops said they weren't qualified to know if I needed medical care. So the EMS people had to come and make sure I was all right before they released me. Released me for the whole block to see. Felt like I was on display. I could feel heat rising up the back of my neck when I walked up our steps and into the house. Everybody probably could tell that too.

Pops and Mr. Glover talked to the cops for a long time before everything settled down. I heard snatches about the mallet. Everybody was upset about the mallet. *Where'd he*

get it? What was he doing with it? He could hurt somebody
with it.

"They say the kid plays polo," one of the cops said into
his radio. "Where? How the heck do I know?"

"In Fairmount Park," said Mr. Glover. "He plays through
one of your affiliations."

"Polo, really?"

"He works with horses in the park . . ." Pops was trying
hard not to get upset again. I could hear it in his voice. "Since
when is that illegal?"

I took a shower and laid down across my bed. Faked like
I was asleep when Grandmom came to check on me. I curled
up in a little ball like I did after my mom first died. Couldn't
even walk down my own street. Stay out of trouble. Isn't that
what Winston and Dre and them said? I got into trouble just
from thinking. Thinking about Foster and Blanchard and
how come the two of them couldn't go together. I didn't do
nothing, but Winston was hooked up with the cops. They'd
probably tell him something about me. Tell him something
so I wouldn't see Chance anymore.

Foster sent me a text: *u ok*? How was I supposed to answer
that? We used to like all the same things. Said he didn't like
being around phony people. Yeah, but what about the horses?
How could he not be down with them?

I sat up in bed and rubbed my stiff neck. The street was
quiet but I couldn't stay still. I got out of bed and turned on

the computer. Found some polo videos, videos with guys and horses running fast and free. I watched them until the sun came up.

GRANDMOM DIDN'T WANT me to go outside the next day. Pops spent over an hour talking to her about it. You can't live your life hiding in the house, just gotta know how to handle yourself in the street. Pops kept saying it wasn't my fault but running around with a mallet wasn't smart. You can't give the cops a reason to get excited.

It was Sunday and I wanted to get over to the stables. I thought Pops was cool, but he wouldn't let me ride my bike over to the park. He and Uncle Ronnie drove me in the car. I wanted them to drop me off a half mile away but Pops wanted to talk to Winston.

It figures Jerome was there when we pulled up. He was all helpful, directing Pops and Uncle Ronnie to Winston's office. He could be two-faced like that. They went inside and left me standing under the big tree in the parking lot with him.

"Where's your boy?" he said. "Sleeping off last night's buzz, no doubt." His mouth was twisted real ugly. "Isn't that how y'all do it 'round the way?"

"I wouldn't know," I said.

"Oh, I forgot. You're past all that now. On the road to respectability."

"You must be talking about yourself." I looked past him and saw some kids already busy with their horses.

"I'm talking about you," he said. "You with the bobos and the played-out jeans. Got yourself in trouble again?"

"You spending a lot of time in my business, Jerome." I looked him right in his face. "What's up with that?"

"I don't know how you think you're gonna play polo when you faint every time somebody touches you," he said. "Just don't go believing all that stuff Winston's been telling you. There's no way you're going to play in exhibition."

"Can't handle a little competition?" I said, walking past him.

"Just watch yourself," he called out after me. He didn't need to tell me to watch myself. I wasn't letting my guard down again.

Some of the horses had already been turned out in the far field. They were standing in a clump, eating from a bale of hay. It didn't look like anything was going on, but if you really looked, you could see there was. Some horses wouldn't move from their spot, no matter what. They didn't let any other horse get between them and the hay. Others didn't seem to have a place. They kept trying to work their way in wherever they could. Horses weren't so different from people.

I was sitting on the top bar of the fence, still watching the horses, when Pops and Uncle Ronnie came back outside. They looked all around, trying to figure out where they were.

That must have been how I looked when I first started coming here. It was easy to get turned around with all the doors and pathways. I waved my hands over my head so they could see me.

"These are beautiful animals," said Pops when they got to me. He put his hands on his hips and looked out over the whole place like he was dreaming. "I wish I could stay here with you."

"Hmm," said Uncle Ronnie, scrolling through messages on his cell. "I got a brunch date."

That snapped Pops out of his dream. He put one hand on my shoulder again. "Winston understands none of this was your fault. And don't worry about getting home. Winston'll drive you."

Uncle Ronnie looked up from his cell. "Give me a quick tour of the place while I'm here. Ugh, it sure does smell."

Pops shook his head. Uncle Ronnie overdid the cologne. That was worse than the horse smell.

"You gotta see Chance," I said, leading them on the path that led to the other side of the barn. I wanted to be close to her.

We saw Alisha with her horse in the cross ties. She was cleaning her horse's face but she waved at me.

"Hold up, hold up," said Uncle Ronnie, stopping dead in his tracks. "I should've known there was a female involved."

"How'd you know Chance is female?" I said.

Uncle Ronnie peered at me over his sunglasses. "Very funny. I just hope I don't mess up my shoes in all this dirt."

I DIDN'T REALLY feel like talking to nobody after they left, not Winston, not Alisha, nobody. I missed Foster, though. Still couldn't believe he wouldn't get with the horses. I cleaned the stalls and then spent a long time brushing Chance. I stayed with her 'cause I didn't want to have to answer anybody's questions. Funny, she kept nudging me with her head, like she had questions.

Pops said the horses were beautiful. He was right about that. It wasn't just the good-looking kind of beauty, either. It had more to do with the way they were, their soul or something. Winston called it grace. Whatever it was, it felt like Chance knew something was wrong with me.

"You may want to be a little softer with her," Winston said, walking over. He'd finished his riding class with two ladies, new students.

"They're so majestic," I overheard one of the ladies say. "I forget all my problems when I'm here."

They walked down the aisle, looking at all the horses. You could tell they weren't used to being in a barn; they jumped every time a horse snorted.

"Feel like taking a ride?" Winston had his car keys in his hand. "I'll take you home."

He waited for me to walk Chance back to her stall. I thought about what that lady had said. She forgot all her problems when she was here. She better be careful about that.

"How are you feeling?" asked Winston.

"Everything's cool," I said, sighing.

Winston's little sports car was parked right next to the barn. I walked around to the passenger side and got in. I'd been hoping to get a ride in his car, but that day, I didn't really care. He started the engine and we drove behind the barn and onto the road.

The fields near the stables were filled with kids playing softball and soccer. Some of them turned to check out the car when we drove past. I wasn't even into that.

"We're lucky to live in a city with a park like this," Winston said, looking all around.

What was he saying? We lived in a city where I couldn't even walk down the street. I didn't say nothing.

"Lived here all your life?"

"Yup."

"Me too," he said. "Born and raised in Philly."

Okay, so I was gonna get his life story. Maybe I could just snooze through it. Somebody wake me up when he gets to the part about horses.

"You know you remind me of myself," he said. Why I'm

always reminding older dudes of themselves, I don't know. Uncle Ronnie's one; Winston makes two. Who's gonna pop up next? Winston had on that fly watch of his, though. His hands were on the steering wheel and rays of late-afternoon sun reflected off of it. "Aren't you going to ask why?" he said.

I shrugged. "Okay, why?"

"You're cool, got your own style." Winston was not shy. "Everybody's always testing you"—he guided the steering wheel with the palm of his right hand—"because they want a piece of what you have. They're afraid of you. That's why they want to hold you down." I wasn't saying nothing. "You just have to know what you want and take advantage of every opportunity that comes your way."

He didn't say nothing about the cops. He didn't have to. I knew what he was talking about. "Like with you?" I said.

He nodded. "Exactly. Your talent with the horses could be a path to wherever you want to go."

We'd left the park and were a block away from my house. Everybody, I mean everybody, was checking out Winston's car and who was in it. He took it all in stride.

"Why me?" I said. There were lots of other kids at the stables. I wasn't sure why he was so focused on me.

"Because I know you want to do well."

"How you know that? You got a crystal ball in your saddlebag or something?"

"Don't play dumb with me, Troy." Winston turned the corner onto my block and pulled up in front of the house. "You have to carry yourself like a thug just to get in and out of here." He looked around the block not to put it down; he just looked like somebody who knew it. "You know what it takes to get along. My job is just to help you out however I can."

I couldn't really argue with him, but I had to say something else. "Are you finished with your lecture?"

"Just one more thing. Polo players don't have saddlebags. You're thinking of cowboys."

CHAPTER SIXTEEN

SCHOOL WAS FINALLY OUT. That was the good news. I had major plans for the summer. I was gonna get my riding real tight. And the other stuff, I don't know, I kept it on lockdown. I didn't see much of Foster; there was a curtain between us. That was the bad news.

And, sometimes, everything would be getting on my nerves. I tried to just put it out of my mind, but I couldn't. Used to be, if somebody bumped into me or something, I would just let it go. I couldn't do that now. If somebody even looked at me wrong, I would get mad. And if somebody really did do something wrong, watch out. Like the day Lay-Lay came around trying to collect money for the block party.

Every summer we have a big blowout on the block. We close off the street and everybody just hangs outside eating, playing cards, listening to music. Usually, there's somebody running the whole thing. I don't know why I'm saying usually; it's always Mr. Glover. Anyway, he gets a couple of people to help. They go around and ask everybody to bring something and to chip in for sodas and ice cream.

Well, this one day, I was sitting on the porch, waiting for Grandmom to say it was time to eat. Here comes Lay-Lay, knocking on everybody's door, asking for donations. He had a little jar with a few dollars in it, so everybody would think their neighbors already gave. He must think we're stupid.

First thing I noticed was Lay-Lay waited until Mr. Glover went inside his house to start this mess. He knocked at the house next door to ours, but nobody answered. They probably saw who it was and didn't want to be bothered. Lay-Lay saw me sitting right there, but he didn't say nothing. He walked down the steps and over to our house. I stopped him as soon as he put his big foot on our bottom step.

"Don't even try it," I said.

"I'm collecting for the block party." He said it with a straight face, but everybody knew he could lie like a mug. "Is your grandmom home?"

"Don't come up here," I said. I picked up the red-and-white metal chair and held it in front of me.

"Watcha gonna do about it?" he said. "Faint?"

"Take one more step up here and you'll find out." I wasn't playing. I was ready to throw that big old chair down on his head. He saw that I was strong enough to do it, too.

"Aw, you ain't even worth it." He stepped backward, down to the sidewalk. "We don't want you at the block party anyway." He skipped Mr. Glover's house and tried the people on the other side.

I put the chair back down on the porch and texted Foster to warn him about Lay-Lay's scam.

Foster: *he must think we're stupid.*

Then: *u coming to block party?*

Me: *not sure. depends when i get done at stables.*

Foster: *ask chance nice. maybe she'll let u out.*

I let it go after that. It wasn't like Foster to have so much attitude.

I sat back down on the porch and thought about how it would feel to hurt somebody. I never thought about doing nothing like that before. It was scary. Scary 'cause there was a hard side of me that kept coming out. I couldn't really control it. I knew that because of what happened between me and Percy.

Percy was always around the stables. Looked like he calmed down the horses. Something about horses and goats, I don't know.

So this one day, nothing was going right even before the Percy thing. I had had a hard time with Chance that morning. She wasn't doing what I wanted her to do. Winston said we weren't on the same page. Said maybe we needed to take a break from each other. Anyway, Percy kept running around Chance's stall, so I couldn't do my work. I shooed Percy out a couple times, but soon as I turned around he'd be right back in there. Got on my nerves, for real.

I want to say this right 'cause I didn't really kick him that hard. I mean, you could say he fell up against my foot. I was trying to muck out Chance's stall and Percy sorta got in the way when I backed up the wheelbarrow. He was running around all crazy, bleating. Making that doll-baby crying sound. That's what caught Alisha's attention. I didn't even know she was in the barn, but she must've seen the whole thing. Or enough of it, anyway. She ran over to Percy like the barn was on fire. I didn't know the girl could move that fast.

"What's wrong with you, Troy?" I never heard her so loud before.

"What?"

"What do you mean, what? You just kicked Percy." She was down on one knee, rubbing his side. Her locs were covering most of her face, but even at that angle, she and Percy looked like Beauty and the Beast.

"He's not hurt," I said, pushing the wheelbarrow over to the door.

"You don't know that." She was using this baby voice, all snuggled up with Percy.

"And you don't know that he is," I said. I took the wheelbarrow outside, hoping she'd be gone when I came back. She wasn't.

"Why are you acting like this? Like you're mad at everybody?" she said.

"Girl, please. You're tripping."

"I'm tripping? You're the one acting weird. You've been weird ever since . . ."

"Ever since what?"

She'd put Percy down by then. Like I'd said, he was all right.

"You're not the first person to be stopped by the police," she said.

"Like you would know." I leaned the empty wheelbarrow up against the wall.

"My friend Sloan got stopped up in North Philly last Friday night," she said.

"Preppy Sloan from your school?"

"What does that have to do with it?"

"Answer the question," I said. "Is Sloan one of your rich friends?"

"I don't see what difference that makes."

"So, your little friend was stopped by the cops in a neighborhood where they didn't expect to see him." I rolled my eyes up to the ceiling. "Did they frisk him?"

"No, they just asked him if he was all right."

I closed my eyes. "Alisha," I said. "You have no idea what it's like, do you?"

"Why are you making such a big deal out of this?"

"What was Sloan doing up in North Philly?"

"I don't know." Her voice was real low. "I just know I wouldn't make such a big deal out of it if it happened to me."

"Don't worry," I said, pulling my baseball cap out of my backpack and putting it on with the brim to the side. "I don't think the cops are going to bother you out at Blanchard Pooloo Club." I turned away from her and walked out.

CHANCE MUST HAVE CAUGHT whatever it was Alisha had, 'cause after that, me and her were totally not cool. I couldn't even catch her to tack up for our ride. She just walked off and went the other way when I tried to get close to her. So, I guess I started chasing her. That just made it worse. She was trying to get away from me. Then you're not going to believe what happened.

Jerome walked over to Chance, real calm like. He made sure he came up to her on one side so she could see him and started rubbing Chance's shoulder and stepping back from her. He held up his hand for me to stay back. I mean, I don't want to blow it up more than it was. He didn't save my life or nothing, but he did chill things out.

"Thanks, man," I said. "She's uptight today."

"Ain't nothing to it," he said, shrugging like this was an everyday thing. He walked Chance a little bit farther away from where I was standing and let her go. She went back over to the other horses in the yard.

I didn't try to run after Chance anymore. I just let her stay with the other horses. Everybody else was going about their business, but I didn't know what to do. So I just upped and left, something that definitely wasn't cool. Everybody was supposed to check in and out with Winston. I don't know, I just had to get out of there. Couldn't stand the way Jerome was strutting around like he was in charge of me.

Real fast, I jumped on my bike and started pedaling like a fool. I took that turn from the parking lot to the street so hard my bike skidded over to the curb. I didn't fall off, though, just straightened it up and kept going.

I shot past the soccer fields, went down past where they play softball and that big swimming pool. Almost ran over these little kids running around in their too-big T-shirts.

I hooked a left at the third intersection instead of going right. Right would have been the way to double back to go home. But, I don't know why, I went left. The road went a little ways before it ended. Pedaling real fast, I went straight up over the grass and into the woods.

Blam! It was like going from day to night. There was hardly any sunlight and it was real quiet. It was different from my walks in the woods in the wintertime. Back then, there weren't any leaves on the trees, so you could see the sky. Now the leaves made everything look dark. I couldn't hear no kids, no traffic, nothing. I was in the middle of all these tall trees with nobody else around. I was in the middle of Philly, but it didn't even smell like the city no more. Christmas trees, that's what it smelled like.

It was hard to control the bike 'cause I wasn't on a trail or nothing. The bike was bumping over roots and leaves and stuff. My hoodie kept getting caught on bushes, but I didn't let that stop me. I just kept going. Then I saw that the woods sloped downward, down to this creek. I tried to slow down but the bike was jumping all over the place. Next thing I knew, my bike was going one way and I was going the other. For a minute it felt like I was in a movie, in a freeze-frame, but then I slipped on some wet leaves and slid on my butt straight down into the creek. It was a miracle I didn't jack myself up.

My pants were wet, but luckily, my rubber boots kept my feet dry. I walked to the other side of the creek; that's where I found my bike. It was totally busted. It didn't have a seat anymore and the front wheel was bent. I just left it there.

I didn't know where I was, just somewhere in the park. Then I remembered I left my cell in my backpack and my backpack was still at the stables, so I couldn't even call nobody. I had to pull myself up, grabbing on to tree branches and stuff just to get up to flat ground.

That's when I sat down. I pulled my hoodie up on my head to keep the gnats away. I crawled over to this opening in a real tall tree. Buried myself in that tree for a long time, trying to figure everything out. You know, I thought I was way over being scared of Chance, but that wasn't true. I was scared she didn't want to be my horse anymore. Scared I was gonna lose her forever.

I don't know how long I stayed there. I must've fallen asleep 'cause when I woke up it was starting to get dark and the trees were creepy-looking. Plus, I was hungry. I wasn't no nature boy, so I couldn't pick berries or, you know, get a fish out of the creek. All I knew was I didn't want to be in the woods after it really got dark. So, I just started walking back the same way I came. Tried to think up a story for Pops. Yeah right.

CHAPTER SEVENTEEN

I HAD TO WALK most of the way home. It took me forever to even get out of the woods. Then, after that, I had to make it back to the intersection where I went left instead of right. I was at the edge of Fairmount Park when I heard a car horn honking. It was my neighbor Mr. Glover.

"Are you all right? Everyone's been out looking for you." He pulled over to the curb under a streetlight and leaned over to open the passenger-side door. I just nodded and dropped down into the seat. I didn't really feel like talking. I was tired. I was hungry. I was wet.

"I'll call your dad so he'll know you're with me." Mr. Glover handed me a bottle of water while he dialed Pops's number.

"Good news, Dave. I'm here with Troy. He's fine." Pops said something that I couldn't hear and then Mr. Glover said okay and hung up.

"You look like you could use a few minutes to collect yourself," he said. He hadn't started the car yet.

"Today just got out of control," I said, looking out the window.

"You're going to have to do better than that," he said. "The man from your riding program—"

"Winston?" I cut in.

"Yes, Winston. He called your dad when he realized you'd left the stables without checking out. He was very concerned and, let's just say, your dad and grandmother have been worried."

"Great." I groaned and slid down lower in my seat.

"Your uncle Ronnie's combing the streets on his Suzuki. Your dad checked with Miss T and Foster, but they didn't know where you were. What's this about you having trouble with your horse?"

"Who said that?"

"Winston."

"So everybody's been talking about me all day?" I sorta shouted 'cause I was pissed off.

"Take it easy. You can't just disappear and show up looking like the Wreck of the Hesperus." Typical Mr. Glover. I caught a look at myself in the side-view mirror. I did look bad. Twigs and leaves were stuck in my hair, my hoodie was poked with holes, and I had a big scratch across my right cheek.

"It's a long story. I got lost in the woods and wiped out my bike."

"What were you doing in the woods?" Without waiting for an answer, he went on. "With all due respect, Troy, this is not your finest moment. Why didn't you call home?"

"'Cause my cell's in my backpack."

"I thought you young people never put those things down," he said.

"I forgot to take it with me when I left the stables." I'd stopped carrying mine around the stables after it fell in the muck. Besides, I didn't like to be bothered when I was with Chance. Mr. Glover kept talking.

"Your dad was going to call the police if you weren't home by ten."

"What for? So they can beat me up again?" My stomach tightened and it all came back. I could feel my face pressed down against the hood of the cop car. Everybody on the block saw me laid out there. Everybody.

"Troy, I know that wasn't an easy thing," Mr. Glover said. It was dark by then. The streetlight shone on Mr. Glover and for the first time I saw how much gray he had in his wiry hair. "We all admired how you carried yourself with dignity during that encounter."

"Some dignity," I said. "I passed out."

"Everybody talks about how you didn't let that ugly incident stifle your spirit. And that's a hard thing to do."

I'd fooled everybody. They didn't know I'd shrunk a little inside. Funny, I couldn't hide that from Chance.

"I better get you home," Mr. Glover said as he started the car. I realized then that I'd never seen him off the block before. He never left his post in the hood, but he did for me.

CHAPTER EIGHTEEN

I GOTTA HAND it to Pops. He didn't go off when I got home. First, he made sure I was all right. Then he asked me what happened, real calm like. Grandmom gave me something to eat and then I took a shower.

This was hard. I didn't have a good story, but I figured I could act out if Pops did. He wasn't going to let that happen. Real smart.

He knocked on my door before I went to bed. He came inside, closed the door, and leaned up against it.

"Troy, do you have any idea what you put us through today?" His shoulders were slumped and I saw the dark circles under his eyes. I didn't say anything 'cause, really, I didn't know what to say. Pops had been looking better the past few weeks, but that night, I saw him slipping backward. He needed that door to hold himself up.

"I'll save some money and buy myself a new bike," I said real fast.

He sighed. "It's not the bike I'm worried about. It's you and the riding program." Pops looked so tired, like it took all his energy just to keep talking. "Winston and Dre are responsible for you during the day. They can't have kids in the program who don't follow the rules."

I hadn't thought about that. Exactly what he was saying.

"What's going to happen now? Am I kicked out?"

"You're not kicked out, but your behavior is a problem. There can't be a repeat of today."

It would have been easier if he had shouted at me, or grounded me, or even cut off my allowance. This was way harder. He was treating me like an adult. We looked at each other; we both knew I'd screwed up. I didn't want to lose Chance and I didn't want to make Pops sad again, either.

"I don't know," I said. "Everything's . . . everything's just real messed up."

"What do you mean?" He walked over to my desk and leaned against it. "I thought you loved being around the horses."

"I do, but . . ." I looked at the horse poster Grandmom bought me. "I haven't been feeling too good lately."

"Are you sick? Why didn't you say something?"

"It's not like a stomachache or nothing." I walked to the window and pulled down the shade so there wasn't any light coming in from the neighbor's house. "I just feel sorta bad all the time . . ."

"When you say bad, do you mean mad?" he said.

I nodded and turned around. "How'd you know?"

"Mad like you could hurt somebody?" He reached down and picked up the mallet I kept propped against the side of my desk. "I know the feeling," he said. "Especially after the cops tried to mess with you."

That's when I told him everything. I told him about being mad and kicking Percy. Being mad and arguing with Alisha. Being mad and struggling with Chance.

Then he told me things. How some things in life aren't right or just. That's the word he used. He told me how you have to know who you are and never, ever let anybody convince you you're not whatever that is. He told me how biking was the way he let off steam, although he never went crazy in no park like I did. And I told him that horses were my magic. How it felt like my mom was with me when I was riding. Funny, he said, he had the same feeling. He'd felt my mom's presence in the park that day, too. Neither one of us wanted to lose that.

CHAPTER NINETEEN

IT WAS FULL-BLOWN SUMMER after that. I don't know, something about being out in Fairmount Park by myself that day helped me deal with stuff. Or, maybe, it was seeing how me being hard was making Chance hard. And me being hard was making Pops sad again. Winston had told me I had to have heart to be good with the horses. I needed it for people, too. Real heart, not the phony kind I'd tried to run down on everybody.

Turns out, I didn't get kicked out of the riding program. Me and Pops had to meet with Winston and Dre. Winston said I would be suspended if I broke the rules again. Said that would be a shame 'cause I had a special touch with the animals. I was glad to hear that 'cause I was afraid Alisha told everybody about me and Percy. She hadn't.

Pops said I would have to contribute half the money for a new bike but, in the meantime, he let me use his.

The toughest part was getting right with Chance.

Winston had me taking care of her again but it was going real slow. Felt like she had to get used to me all over again. I planned to talk to Dre about it 'cause I was feeling lonely, too. I ain't gonna lie; I was missing Foster tough. We weren't hanging out 'cause he was doing something with the basketball league. And I didn't mean to, but I missed the block party. Well, maybe I could have caught the last part of it, but by the time I got home from the stables, Mr. Glover was breaking things down so the street could reopen to traffic.

"I saved you a slice of Miss T's blueberry pie," he called over his shoulder when he saw me coming around the corner. "You owe me big-time." The highlight of the block party was always Miss T's pies. Folks waited all year for them.

"Thanks," I said, looking around at the balloons that were still tied to the backs of some of the folding chairs. "How'd everything go?"

"Great, as always." He straightened up and put his hands on his hips. "You can still catch up with some of the kids," he chuckled. "They're having a little after-party over at Foster's. Club Parachute they're calling it."

"Club Parachute?" So Foster's room was open to everybody now? Used to be that spot was just for us. "I'm sorta tired now," I said. "I think I'll . . ."

"Hold on a minute," said Mr. Glover. "Let me go get the pie before I accidentally eat it." He stopped to look at me. "You okay?" he said.

"Yeah, just tired." I faked a big stretch so he wouldn't keep asking questions.

WHEN I WASN'T at the stables, I spent most of my time on the Internet watching polo videos and reading all about horses. The videos all said you had to have the right attitude. Being slick or mean wouldn't work with the animals. I didn't want to be corny like Dre, but he lived with all the horses. I knew he'd have good advice.

I was looking for him the next day but I just had to stop to watch the polo players doing their stick-and-ball practice. That's where you ride around the field and hit the ball. It sounds nice and easy, but it isn't. You gotta control your horse and practice your swings at the same time. It was hot and the horses were kicking up a lot of dust. Our polo field was dirt, not nice grass like out at Blanchard.

All the players looked good but you could see Jerome was the best. He could hit the ball long distances, longer than any of the other players. They all knocked the ball up and down the field like there was nothing to it. And they all had their own style. Each dude had his own way of showing his stuff. Same as in b-ball.

They ended their practice, and Willie and Little Keith walked their horses over to the hose. Jerome and Marcus walked their horses toward me. I wiped my forehead with the bottom of my T-shirt. I wasn't really feeling Jerome. I was tired of all the fronting that went along with being around him but Marcus saw me and waved.

"What's going on?" he said when he got to the railing where I was standing. I hadn't stopped him; he spoke to me first. Jerome kept walking. Good.

"I'm looking for Dre," I said. I couldn't help but add, "You guys looked great."

Jerome had already passed, but he had to turn and shout over his shoulder. "Better than you ever will." Marcus rolled his eyes and shook his head. "Marcus," Jerome said. "Are you coming or you gonna waste your time with him?"

"Why you sweating me?" said Marcus. "I'll catch up with you." He waved Jerome off.

Marcus and his horse were both dusty but the shine from his horse's coat still peeked out in between the patches of dirt. "I gotta take care of him," he said, looking at his horse, "but, you know, I'm going to be leaving soon. I just wanted to tell you to hang in there." I hoped he wouldn't mention the cops. "I've seen you and Chance together; you definitely got something going on."

"Well, we're having some problems now," I said.

"I'm not worried; you'll straighten it out." Marcus patted his horse. "Winston's already counting on you to play at exhibition."

"I haven't been riding that long."

"You've got something special," said Marcus. "Don't worry, Winston'll help you along."

Marcus led his horse away. I kept thinking about what he'd said. *You've got something special.* That's what everybody kept saying but I didn't really know what that meant anymore.

DRE WAS INSIDE, gathering up some medicine he needed for one of the horses.

"How's things going with Chance?" he said.

"That's what I came to talk to you about."

"Isn't Winston helping you with that?"

"He is, but it's going slow."

"It all comes down to trust," Dre said. "Don't try to rush it. Just be honest with your animal." He checked some papers on his desk before looking back up at me. "They don't like ugly." Horses weren't the only ones who didn't like ugly; I didn't, either. "You're bigger than that," Dre went on to say. "Deal with it when you have to, but that isn't the real you."

That's sorta what Pops had said. Seemed like everybody went through some bad stuff sooner or later but you couldn't let it bring you down. I wondered what Jerome had to deal with. Must have been pretty bad to make him the way he was.

"Well," I said, "I found some videos about how to get back with your horse."

"Check you out," Dre said, smiling. "Smart to do your own research. Let me take care of this new horse. She's not feeling too good. After that, I'll have some time to talk."

Dre knew the horse wasn't feeling too good. I'm sure he could tell I wasn't feeling too good, either.

CHAPTER TWENTY

FOSTER WAS ON MY MIND when I woke up. Usually, it was Chance, but this time it was my boy. I just wanted everything to be good again, like it was before we went out to Blanchard, before I came home and let my guard down.

Winston and Dre kept telling me you can't fake it with horses. They can tell when you're all twisted up inside. Well, I was over trying to be slick but I still had to find a place inside my brain for that cop thing.

Chance was out in the field rolling around on her back when I got to the stables the next morning. I remembered how surprised I'd been the first time I saw a horse do that. Now I knew she was just scratching herself.

I'd just finished mucking out her stall when I saw Alisha standing in the open doorway. Hadn't really talked to her since our argument. It wasn't like I was avoiding her or nothing. Just seemed like our paths hadn't crossed. That was funny, though, since the place wasn't that big.

She was standing there looking up at the sky. It wasn't hot yet 'cause the sun was just getting to the top of the trees. When I walked toward her, I could smell the fresh air coming through the open door. You know, that smell when you're outside early in the morning. You can't smell it on the block, but it's there in the park.

"What are you looking at?" I said, walking up behind her. She put her finger to her lips to shush me, and a really big bird took off from a tree in front of the barn. She shielded her eyes with one hand and pointed at the bird with the other.

"A hawk," she said. "That's why all the little birds disappeared."

"You sure do know a lot about nature," I said.

"It's not hard. You just need to open your eyes to what's around you." That was easy to do here with the trees and grass and all. Harder to do when I was anyplace else. "I think Chance misses you," she said. She dropped her hand and looked at me. I could tell she wanted to say something else, but she let it go. I'm glad 'cause I didn't want to get choked up or nothing. "Uncle Winston tells me you're further along with her than you think."

"We'll see," I said. "I'm gonna let my girlfriend tell me herself."

Alisha laughed and turned to head inside. "Oh, I almost forgot. I'm having a party in a couple of weeks. Hope you can come."

"Who else is gonna be there?"

"Kids from here and some from my school. You'll get an invitation."

"An invitation? Sounds fancy."

"It's not. That's just Uncle Winston's way of doing things." She saw the look on my face. "Don't worry. It's not going to be all like that. It'll be fun."

Other kids had arrived at the stables by then. I walked over to the field to get a closer look at Chance. She was back up on her feet, so I went over to her. I could see her skin rippling as she tried to shake off some flies. I didn't try to grab her or nothing. Just let her look at me, smell me. Maybe that was the way to do it. She starting walking around me, so I did the same thing. I walked around her. We were sorta circling each other. I wasn't chasing her. Just walking slow. That's when it hit me. The horse smell didn't bother me anymore. Winston said it would happen sooner or later; here it was.

Chance stopped, so I stopped. The only thing moving was her swishing tail. Next thing I knew, she took one little step toward me. I didn't want to crowd her, so I took one step back. Then we walked around each other again. I just stayed loose like I did the first day I rode her. We kept going like this until we were coming to each other, not stepping back. Felt like she could see right through me with those big eyes of hers. When Chance was close enough for me to reach, I rubbed her neck. She didn't act out. I didn't, either. I wished that everything could feel just like that all the time. I was petting her when Winston came over.

"Good job," he said, putting his arm across my shoulders. "You have just the right touch."

"Yeah, well, it took me long enough," I said.

"Don't put yourself down," he said. "There are other people to do that."

I let Chance go then. She didn't run away, just took her time walking back over to the other horses.

"She'll let you ride her whenever you want," he said. I shook my head yeah. "I've been meaning to talk to you." I saw that he was starting to sweat. "It's gotten really hot out here; let's pull up some shade."

We walked over to the other side of the barn. The shadows made it cooler. Over in the far field, the polo team was going through their drills. "As I was saying, I think you're talented," said Winston. "I hope you're planning to get serious about all of this."

"What?" I said. "About Chance?"

He nodded. "Chance, riding, and polo. I want you to play in the exhibition match."

"What about my problems with Chance?"

"Everybody goes through something like that at one point or another. The important thing is how you come out of it."

I should have told him that I still had a lot of other stuff to figure out, too.

"I saw you with her just now. That was pure magic. So, think about it. I'd be happy to start coaching you for more extensive riding and for polo. Of course, you'll need to get your dad's permission. It'll be a lot of work. He has to be on board."

This was coming at me out of the blue. "Okay," I said.

"Okay? Is that all you have to say?" He swatted his hand at me. I ducked and we both laughed. "We're going to have one powerhouse team at exhibition," he said, playing with his watch. "I was worried that after Marcus left we'd be in trouble." He was talking to himself. "But we'll be okay. We'll be more than okay. It's going to be a lot of work." He'd said that before. "I was afraid you and Jerome couldn't work together, but I saw how he helped you out with Chance. We're going to be great."

"Me and Jerome?" I said.

"Yes. You, Jerome, Willie, and Little Keith."

"So, you think everything's cool between me and Jerome?"

"Yes," he repeated. "He helped you the day you took off, remember?"

I sure remembered that day. It wasn't the way Winston saw it. It was never like that. Jerome didn't help me because he was my friend. He only stepped in to make himself look good.

"I know he gave you a hard time when you first got here," Winston said. "He's like that with everybody. He's just insecure, afraid of losing his place."

His place? Jerome's bad news. What was Winston saying? Something about not wanting to share the limelight. Oh boy.

"You'll be at Alisha's party, won't you?" he said. "There's a lot of people you need to meet."

"What kind of party is it gonna be?" He started telling me who all was going to be there and all like that. I had a feeling this wasn't gonna be like the parties I usually went to. This was gonna be something else.

CHAPTER TWENTY-ONE

THE REST OF THAT DAY was like a blur. Winston gave me books about polo and showed me all this equipment I was gonna have to get used to—goggles, a polo saddle, bandages to protect the horse's legs, and special boots for their hooves. He wasn't even waiting for me to go home and talk to Pops. He was all over it like everything was already cool. Felt like I was being drafted for the NBA or something. Don't get me wrong. It was great that he wanted to coach me, but he was way off on the Jerome thing.

I took a shortcut home 'cause I was so excited. Came around the corner and saw Grandmom's friend, Miss Evelyn, helping her up the front steps. At first, I didn't recognize them. Grandmom was wearing pink sweats. Her feet looked like they were about a size two in her Nikes. She would've looked cool, except she wasn't walking right.

"I'm glad you're home," Miss Evelyn said when I pulled

up on Pops's bike. She was dressed the same way. "Your nana's going to need some help."

"What happened?" I carried the bike up to the porch, squeezing past them on the steps.

"She's overextended herself—"

"Evelyn, you never could tell a good story," Grandmom interrupted her with a sigh. "I won the Zumba dance-off. That's what happened."

"You?" I said.

"Yes, me." Grandmom straightened herself up. "Now I'm feeling it."

She made it up to the porch and sat down, fanning herself. Miss Evelyn leaned up against the railing.

"Troy, will you get her a glass of water?" she said.

I got Grandmom's favorite glass, the one from Hershey with the kisses all over it, and filled it with water. I went back out to the porch and handed it to her.

"Our exercise class at the senior center got these new students," Grandmom said. "Two women who moved down here from New York. They thought they were the only ones who could dance. Well, I showed them."

"I didn't like their attitude from the beginning," said Miss Evelyn, squinching up her face. "Taking the best spots in class, hogging our instructor's time. We've been in the class all along. They've only been here a few weeks."

"Acting like they owned the place," said Grandmom. "Even brought their own music, like ours wasn't good enough."

"They were the ones who suggested the dance-off." Miss Evelyn leaned forward, with her hands on her hips. "They thought they could win. Well, they thought wrong."

"I didn't know you were so competitive," I said.

"I'm not," said Grandmom, "but I had to rep-re-sent." She drew it all out like she knew what she was talking about.

"You should have seen her, Troy." Miss Evelyn snapped her fingers three times. "She was a dancing machine."

That's when Miss Evelyn really got me. She pushed off the railing and switched across the porch. Then she switched back and broke into this old-school, James Brown kinda thing. I lost it. For real.

"That's Zumba?" I said when I could stop laughing enough to get it out.

"I was asking myself the same thing," said Miss Evelyn, "but nobody could keep up with her." She was chuckling and fanning herself, too. "How's things with the horses, Troy?"

"Great," I said. "Winston wants to coach me for polo."

"I'm not surprised. You can do whatever you set your mind to." She turned to Grandmom and cupped her hand over her mouth. "What's polo, Louise?"

"I'll explain it to you if you help me get into a hot bath," said Grandmom, stretching from side to side in her chair. "I can't make dinner tonight, Troy. You and your dad are going to have to fend for yourselves."

I held the screen door for them and they went inside. They were going up the steps when I heard Grandmom explain that you had to be a really good rider and have good hand-eye coordination to bang a ball down a field while you were hanging off a horse. It was funny to hear her describe it like that, but she was right.

I was finishing off the water in Grandmom's glass when Pops pulled onto the block. He parked the car in a spot a few doors down and walked over to the house. He looked tired but the Hershey's glass cheered him up.

"I didn't know we still had those," he said. My mom was the one who bought the glasses when she chaperoned my fourth-grade class on a school trip.

"This is the last one. The others broke a long time ago."

"Wonder what we're having for dinner tonight," he said, reaching for the screen door.

"That depends on you. Grandmom's off duty."

He shook his head when I told him the story. "As long as she's having fun," he said. "I know how to make two things: oatmeal and grilled cheese sandwiches."

"It's too late for oatmeal."

"Or we could get a pizza," he said. "There's that place that's always sliding their menus under the door. Give me a minute to check on Grandmom."

"I'll be in my room."

I followed him into the house, put the bike in the basement, and went upstairs. When I turned on the computer, there was an email from Alisha. An Evite with a picture of a horse. The party was at her house, someplace down in Society Hill. Someplace we never went. I didn't even know people lived there.

I looked to see who else was invited. Not many kids I knew. It figured that Jerome already said he'd be there. I checked for Foster's name. Good, he was invited even though he wasn't around the stables anymore.

Pops came into my room and told me Grandmom was okay, just sore.

"You feel like some pizza?" he asked, looking over my shoulder at the Evite.

"Where's Head House Square?" I said.

"That's down in Society Hill. You've been invited to a party down there?" He leaned over to get a closer look at the Evite. Their house was near the square, on one of those tiny little streets that only run one block.

"Yeah. Winston and Alisha are having something."

"I'll say. That's a something address. Down in the Historic District."

"Maybe I'll meet some polo players," I said. I remembered how cool they looked out at Blanchard. "And guess what else happened today."

"The Phillies made it to the play-offs?" Pops shrugged.

"Close," I said. "Winston wants to give me private riding lessons and he wants to start me on polo, too."

"Wow!" That's all Pops could say for a a few seconds. Then he said it again. "Wow!" He sat down on my bed, still looking like he didn't know what to say. I filled him in.

"It's gonna be a lot of work, so I'm gonna need your approval. I'm gonna need leather boots, not just the rubber ones. And I'm gonna need gloves and knee pads, too."

"This is great," he said, "but how much is all this going to cost?"

"Winston's not gonna charge us for the lessons. He thinks I can really be good."

"Did he say that?" he asked.

I nodded. Pops broke out in a grin.

"I don't need a new bike. We can use the money for the polo stuff," I said.

Pops waved his hand. "We'll get the money together." He grinned at me again. "Sounds like he's investing in you. Are you sure this is what you want?"

That was Pops's way of asking if I was ready to stop fooling around. Fooling around hadn't been on my mind for a long time. Not since my first ride. Not since that feeling that got me close to my mom. I nodded even though the thing with the cops, that thing that made me mad sometimes, that thing was still there.

"I'll call Winston tomorrow," he said. "Let's go get something to eat."

The pizza place was four blocks from our house, next to the liquor store with all the bars on the windows. Most folks on our street were like Mr. Glover and kept their sidewalk clean. But once we got off the block, it was a different story. Trash, broken bottles, all that junk everywhere. We were crossing the vacant lot behind the storefront church when we saw a stray dog scratching at something in the dirt.

"Watch out for the dog," Pops said. "You never know if he's mean."

"He's probably wondering the same thing about us," I said.

CHAPTER TWENTY-TWO

ME AND CHANCE were right on it the next day, and the next day and the day after that. Seemed like she was happy. I guess 'cause I was happy. Winston didn't waste any time letting everybody know his plans for me and the exhibition match. Everybody was buzzing about it, that and Alisha's party. I couldn't not show down in Society Hill, but I didn't want to go all the way down there by myself. I really needed my boy.

I texted Foster and asked him if I could drop by his house. He said yeah, even though I didn't come to the best block party ever. He didn't say anything about his private party.

It was good to be back up in his room. I took my old spot, sprawled on his beanbag, and watched the fading sunlight shine through the bottom of his parachute. Strands of red, blue, yellow, and purple stretched across the room.

"I'm not going to Alisha's, so don't even ask." He was sitting on top of his desk with his feet on the chair. I could tell he liked having me come to him for help.

"You know, it may not be that bad."

"What makes you think that?" he said. "At Winston's house, how can it not be bad?"

Foster likes to eat, so I tried to use that. "The grub will be good," I said.

He kept going like he didn't hear me. "Did you see who's invited? Jerome, people from Blanchard, kids from fancy schools."

"You sound like you expect George Washington to show," I said. That shut him up but he wasn't really paying attention to me. His cell was pinging like crazy from all the texts he was getting. He didn't tell me who it was. Probably his new basketball friends.

"You know Miss T's bugging me about it," he finally said, sliding off the desk. Good old Miss T. She was always on the case. "She's not making me go," he added. "She knows I'd rather be around here."

"Hanging at the block party?"

"Exactly, man. Just feels more real."

"And the basketball league?"

"Yup." He hesitated. "Everybody's asking about you," he said. "Everybody's wondering if we're still tight."

"Are we?" I hadn't planned on bringing this up, but there it was. The sun had gone down and, except for the computer screen, Foster's room was dark. That made it easier to talk.

"I'm not down with the whole polo thing, you know that, but we're still homies." We nodded at each other in the computer's glow. "Just don't go getting all high and mighty on me." There was that old Foster grin. He slid into his Winston impersonation. Cracked me up.

"There may be some honeys at Alisha's party," I said, trying another tack. "Look at Alisha. She must have some fine friends." That perked him up. "We don't have to stay for the whole thing, either," I said. "We can just check it out."

"We can't just up and leave when we want to. Somebody's gonna have to pick us up."

"It's near Head House Square, near South Street," I said. "If we don't like the party, we can go hang over there."

Foster thought about it for a few seconds. "All right, I'm in," he said, checking his messages again. "Oh, I heard about you and the coaching."

"Yeah," I said. "It's gonna be cool. How'd you hear about it?"

"Your pops told Miss T," he said. "I'll bet Jerome's not too happy about it. Watch out for him, man." By the tone of Foster's voice, I could tell he wasn't too happy about it, either.

CHAPTER TWENTY-THREE

I WAS REALLY busy that next week. Winston made sure I rode Chance every day. Said the best practice for polo was to ride, ride, ride and talk to your horse. Said he wanted me and Chance to be as tight as could be. Shoot, she knew more about me than anybody else, 'cause when I was with her, I'd be talking straight up. And she'd talk back in her own way. You know, she'd neigh and toss her head.

Winston'd been all over the world playing polo. He told me that on one of our long rides. Said if you were really good, you could make a lot of money and a name for yourself. Said he'd gotten his start by working as a stable hand when he was a kid. He never said why he quit the circuit, but it was real important to him to win. He talked a lot about going back out to Blanchard with a killer team. Yeah, he liked to show off. And maybe I did a little showing off, too, especially after Pops got me a pair of leather riding boots. Made me feel like I was the real deal.

So, then it felt like other kids were looking at me different. Like they knew I was gonna play in the match and be the next star. That's all I was thinking about until the day before Alisha's party. I was doing my usual thing, stretching after my ride so I wouldn't be sore, when Jerome came sliding out the barn.

"Somebody get Dre," he said. "Something's wrong with Percy. He can't walk."

One of the kids went for Dre, and me and Winston followed Jerome back into the barn. Percy was all curled up behind the hay, way in the back. He couldn't stand up. He kept trying, but his legs wouldn't hold him. He looked real bad, too. His eyes were all glassy like people on drugs.

Winston cleared some of the hay away so there was more room around Percy. He picked up his head. "Get some water," he said, rubbing Percy's neck.

By then just about everybody, Alisha and all the other kids, were in the barn. Dre came in the side door and almost tripped over Winston.

"I called the vet." Dre was down on his knees, looking in Percy's eyes. "He'll be here in a few minutes." Then he looked in Percy's mouth. He also pulled out one of those things you use to listen to somebody's heart and put it on Percy's chest. You could tell he knew what to do. "Try to get him to take some water," he said.

"I hope nobody tried to poison him." Jerome said that. He handed Winston a bucket of water and stood there looking down at Percy.

"Who would do that?" said Winston. He had this strange expression on his face when he looked up at Jerome. "Why would you even say that?"

"Everybody back up. Give him some room to breathe," said Dre, standing up.

Dre said he'd stay with Percy until the vet came. Winston wanted everybody to get back to what they were doing. That's when I felt somebody's eyes on me. You know when you can feel somebody looking at you. Man, if looks could kill, I'd be dead right now 'cause Alisha was staring me down.

CHAPTER TWENTY-FOUR

ME AND FOSTER wanted to take the bus down to Society Hill, but Miss T wouldn't have it. Said she wasn't going to miss her chance to get inside a fancy house, so she drove us downtown. Pops said he'd pick us up at ten. I didn't really know what to expect. Not after what happened to Percy the day before. I couldn't stop thinking about his glassy eyes. He'd looked so helpless when he couldn't stand up.

So, we were in the car with Miss T, heading downtown, and I was getting nervous. Suppose Percy died? Everybody would blame me. I was looking out the window, not really paying attention to nothing.

"I've always liked the way this is laid out," said Miss T. She turned off the radio like we couldn't look and listen at the same time.

We were on the Benjamin Franklin Parkway. You know, where they have the flags from all the different countries. Everything so clean and neat. She was playing tour guide.

"Let's take Pine Street down to Society Hill," she said. "I haven't been here in ages."

We went down to a circle with a big fountain in the middle. Turned off on a side street, past some office buildings. But, all of a sudden, there were a lot of cars.

"Oh, I forgot about Rittenhouse Square traffic," she said. "There's always something going on down here."

Lots of older kids, mostly white but some black kids, too, were hanging out in the square. There were these signs strung up in the trees. Said a band was gonna be playing later. People were sitting out at little tables on the sidewalk around the square. Real nice.

Miss T ended up getting all twisted up with the traffic. That didn't help my stomach. It was already curling in on itself. I was worried about Percy. Worried about this party with all these rich kids, too. Maybe Dre would be there. He was somebody me and Foster could talk to. We had to go all around the square before we could go east again.

"I hope you guys don't mind the detour," she said, patting Foster's hand.

She took a few more wrong turns before we got to Pine Street. The streets were getting smaller and everything was closer together. We passed all these restaurants with people sitting outside. And there were little stores selling old stuff, antiques. Stuff just looked old to me.

"I don't suppose you guys remember being here, do you?"

She pointed to Pennsylvania Hospital. "That's where you were born, both of you."

The hospital looked like a museum. Most of it was behind a brick wall. And where there wasn't a wall, there was a black iron fence. You could see a statue and gardens and trees and stuff.

A horse pulling a carriage was walking down Fifth Street. That horse didn't look too happy, lonely or something. That horse needed a little goat to keep her company.

"Is that a parking spot?" said Miss T. "That's lucky. I thought I was going to have to just drop you off in front of their house." She pulled into the spot and we walked the few blocks to Winston's. "Glad I didn't wear heels. These cobblestones are slippery and they're not even wet," she said.

Everything was brick. The streets, the sidewalks, the houses, and all these walls. Felt like we were surrounded by brick walls. You couldn't see over them, but you could hear voices coming from the other side.

Good thing Miss T parked the car where she did. Winston's street was so tiny, looked like a car wouldn't be able to drive down it. A lot of the houses had flags. Not just the American flag. Some were blue; some were yellow with a snake on them. And everybody wanted you to know how old their house was. Little stories about the houses were on pieces of paper stuck in the windows. Grandmom and Miss Evelyn probably had stories about the houses on our block, too. They just hadn't written them down.

"I thought Winston would've lived in a big house out in the suburbs," said Foster, "not on no teeny—"

"Shhh." Miss T put her finger to her lips. "You don't know how your voice carries."

There were a lot of trees on Winston's block. Sorta like a picture frame around the street. We were coming up to a group of people in the middle of the block. Mainly kids, but a few adults like Miss T were there, too. There was a guy all dressed in black handing out drinks on Winston's doorstep. Champagne for the adults, sparkling water for the kids.

Miss T smoothed down her dress before we got to the door. She turned around to check me and Foster out for the umpteenth time. We both had on khakis and our dress shoes. I wanted to wear my new Sixers T-shirt, but Grandmom made me wear a shirt with a collar. Foster was all buttoned down. He looked preppy, except the kids who really went to fancy schools had their shirttails hanging out.

The house was narrow, but it went real far back. Wasn't no vestibule or nothing. We just stepped right into a room with a low ceiling with these beams made out of wood holding it up. There was an old wooden table with a big, big, big bunch of flowers on it. Then everything just opened up. You could see through the living room and this real big kitchen to the backyard. That's where the kids were, out in the back.

Looked like everything in the house was wooden or brick, even some of the walls, and there was a fireplace.

I would've known this was Winston's house even if I didn't know it. There were black-and-white pictures of horses and polo players in silver frames on a ledge above the fireplace.

Winston had on that slick polo watch. Couldn't help but notice it when he came over and kissed Miss T two times, once on each cheek.

"I'm glad you could make it," he said. He held Miss T's hand for a little minute. "Can I get you some champagne?"

"I'm just dropping the boys off," she said, smiling. "This is a lovely home. I don't get down to this part of the city very often."

"You're welcome to join us," he said. "The kids are in the garden, but some of my neighbors will be dropping by a little later."

"Thank you, but no," said Miss T. "I really do need to run." Turning to us, she said, "Have fun, you two."

Winston walked her to the door. Miss T wasn't bad-looking. And, yeah, Winston was checking it out. I gotta admit. I didn't want her to leave. She knew how to handle herself.

"Let's check out what they have to eat before we split," said Foster.

We headed out to the backyard. It was brick, too. It was like another room 'cause there wasn't any dirt anywhere. The floor was brick and the walls had little statutes built into them. Big pots with flowers were in the corners and anchored high up on the walls. Music was coming outta these rocks that weren't really rocks; they were speakers. Alisha was in the center of a bunch of kids standing next to a long table with food.

Me and Foster walked over to the table. I tried to catch Alisha's eye, but she acted like she didn't see me. She was busy with her fancy school friends. Okay, it was gonna be like that.

"You were right about the honeys," said Foster, looking around.

He wasn't lying. There was one fine girl beside the next. Nobody was dancing, though. Just standing around eating and talking.

"Don't I know you? You go to Burton, right?" a girl with these big shoes she couldn't walk in said to Foster. She stopped and looked him up and down.

"No," he said. "I know Alisha from the riding program."

"Oh, you must be a derelict polo player." Her eyes were open real wide. She was trying to be cute, but I thought she looked stupid.

"Not really," said Foster. "I just learned how to ride."

"Alisha . . . Alisha," the girl said real loud, "where are the polo players? You said they'd be here."

Alisha looked over at us then. "Girl, chill out," she said. "He's cool."

Oh, so Foster was cool. Not me, huh? "Hey, Alisha," I said, lifting my chin in her direction.

"Hey," she said. Nothing else.

The backyard was getting crowded and somebody turned the music up. There were all kind of kids there—Asian, white, Latino. I hadn't seen Jerome earlier, but there he was, standing in the doorway between the kitchen and the yard with Willie and Little Keith. They were all wearing their polo jerseys, showing off as usual.

I saw Dre in the kitchen. He waved to me to come inside. Foster seemed to be hitting it off with that stupid-looking girl, so I worked my way back inside.

"How's it going?" he asked.

"Pretty good," I lied. I didn't want him to know nobody was talking to me.

"Well, thank goodness Percy's okay." He was leaning into me like it was a secret or something. "He just ate something he shouldn't have." I wondered if he'd told everybody else the good news. "Oh, there's Winston's neighbor," he said, nodding to this old dude in a seersucker suit. "He's the head of one of the best schools in the city. I'll introduce you and Foster before the evening's over."

So that's what this party was for. Nobody's birthday. No dancing. Just meeting people. I looked out into the yard and caught Foster's eye. Thought he'd be ready to go, but he had his plate piled high with food. And he was talking to a different girl.

It was getting dark and the yard lights came on. Some of the girls started singing along to the music; I didn't know the song. That's when I felt something brushing up against my leg. It was a cat. All gray with a real shiny coat. I bent down to scratch the cat behind its ears. When I stood up, Alisha was standing right behind me.

"Let's hope she doesn't get sick, too," she said.

"What are you talking about?"

"You and Percy." She looked like she was gonna cry. "What's wrong with you?"

"Nothing's wrong with me, and Dre just told me Percy's okay." I looked over my shoulder to make sure nobody else could hear. "I kicked Percy but I wouldn't try to hurt him."

"That doesn't even sound right."

"You know what I mean," I said.

"I knew I should have told Uncle Winston and Dre about you."

"I didn't poison Percy."

"Well, who did?"

"Nobody. Dre said he just ate the wrong thing."

"And you just happened to be around?"

"Girl, you make it sound like I'm an ax murderer or something." I turned around again to make sure nobody was near us. "Look, I was mad when I kicked Percy. It only happened once."

"But you're mad all the time," she said. "That's the problem."

"Do I look mad now?"

"You look like the life of the party," she said, dry as could be. "Why can't you be more like Foster? He's fun."

I looked out into the yard. Foster was laughing and bobbing his head to the music.

"So, you didn't say nothing to nobody about me and Percy?" I said.

"No."

"Well, how come Jerome tried to set me up?"

"Nobody can set you up if you didn't do anything." I didn't know where she got that idea, but I just let it go.

"Wait a minute," I said. "Who started all this poison talk in the first place?"

Alisha sighed and looked around the room. "Now you're tripping," she said. "Jerome loves animals. He wouldn't hurt Percy or any of the horses."

"Neither would I," I said. I was for real, too. I was ashamed that I'd ever kicked Percy.

Somebody turned the music up and kids were finally starting to dance. And my boy who didn't want to come, Foster, was all up in it.

"I gotta go," said Alisha.

She went back outside and turned the music down. All the kids groaned. A voice from the other side of the wall said thank you.

My stomach started to growl and I realized I hadn't eaten anything since breakfast. I don't know why I didn't eat. There was plenty of grub but, I don't know, I just wasn't settled enough.

Anyway, the wide-eyed girl, the one who was looking for polo players, wanted to dance. I didn't really feel like it, but it would have been totally uncool to say no. So we were dancing near the table with the food and she spills her soda all over the bricks. The girl wasn't drunk 'cause they weren't serving alcohol to kids. It was nothing like that. But it looked like she wanted everybody to think she was drunk. How do I know, she may have gotten her buzz on before she came to the party. Anyway, the bricks were wet and I was dizzy 'cause, like I said, I hadn't eaten. This girl was hanging all over me and I had on my dress shoes, okay?

Next thing I know, we're on the bricks. I couldn't get up 'cause the girl was in my way. I looked up and all I could see were those brick walls closing in. Bricks pressing into my back and I couldn't get up.

"I hope you play polo better than you dance." Jerome was standing over us, laughing.

I felt my checks burning just like the other time I was laid out in front of everybody. I couldn't do nothing to that cop, but I could do something now.

Jerome was looking around to see who was laughing at his joke. That's when I stuck my foot out and tripped him up. He tried to catch himself but he was off balance. Yup, he crashed right into the table. Everything went flying, food everywhere.

Nobody else could tell how he tripped. It was dark. He could have caught his foot on the girl's shoes. They were big enough. But he knew it was me.

"You don't know who you're messing with," he said. The girl was looking for her shoes. Me and Jerome were staring each other down.

"What's that supposed to mean?" Winston was between us, in the middle of the food and broken plates.

The music was off and everybody was just standing there. Dre started hustling kids out of the yard, back into the house.

"I don't know how this got started," Winston said, "but it's over. Have I made myself clear?"

"I'm cool," I said, but Jerome didn't say nothing.

Alisha was surrounded by all her girlfriends, crying for real now. "Thanks for ruining my party," she said.

Winston was totally pissed. He looked around at the mess. There wasn't nothing left that you could eat. He almost slipped on the bricks himself.

"I'm sorry, but we're going to have to end the evening." That's all he said.

I looked around to find Foster. He was getting some girl's

number. Left it to me to call Pops and ask him to come pick us up early.

Some of the kids were heading over to this other dude's house to keep the party going. I figured I wouldn't know the words to any of the songs over there any more than I knew them at Alisha's. So me and Foster left the party right after Winston told everybody to get out. Well, you know Winston, he didn't say it like that. How'd he put it? *We're going to have to end the evening.* Same thing.

I lied to Dre and told him Pops was waiting for us over at Head House Square. It wasn't a total lie. Pops was on his way down, just wasn't there yet.

We were hanging over at Head House counting all the piercings on South Street kids. Foster was texting Niki, one of the girls he met.

"You seem pretty into that girl," I said.

"She's all right." He was busy with his cell. Then a minute later: "What were you and Alisha talking about? She didn't look too happy."

"You wouldn't be happy, either, if your party got turned out."

"No, before that. She wasn't happy even before the circus act." So, I was a clown now?

"She thinks I got it in for Percy," I said.

"Why would she think that?"

"I don't know," I said. "Jerome trying to start something."

"I think he got hurt when he fell," he said. "He was limping when he left the party."

"Probably just trying to get some sympathy from that girl he was talking to."

"No, I think he was really hurt."

Nobody could prove I'd tripped him. I tried changing the subject. "Did you see Winston checking out Miss T?"

Foster looked up from his cell. "I missed that," he said.

Now, that was hard to believe. Foster didn't miss anything. "You ain't do too bad yourself," I said. "How many numbers did you get?"

"Only Niki's. Wasn't looking to collect numbers."

"Could've fooled me," I said. "I was ready to leave a while ago, but you were busy with all those girls."

"What, all those girls?"

"I'm just saying, nothing would have gone down if we'd left earlier."

Foster looked away, toward South Street. "You know something, Troy. I'm tired of playing your little sidekick."

"Sidekick? You're the one who said we should leave after we ate."

"Yeah, well, I changed my mind." He jammed his cell into his pocket. "If that's okay with you."

"Well, you could have said something instead of just dumping me."

154

"Look who's talking about dumping." His mouth hung open. "You're the one who doesn't have time for the block party, or me, or anything else." His eyes bore into me real hard. "I only came down here to help you out."

"Help me out?" I shouted. "Since when you gotta help me out?" People on the street were turning to look at us.

"You think that horse is everything," he said, shaking his head. "Well, I got my own stuff."

"Like what?" I laughed. "Your parachute party?"

"Parachute . . ." Foster mouthed the word before he stepped off the curb, looking for Pops's car. "Nobody missed you at my party, man. And you know what else? Everybody knew how to act . . . how to mingle."

"Is that what you call it?" I said.

Foster shook his head as Pops pulled up to the curb. "Seriously, man. You used to be cool. What happened?"

I couldn't answer my boy. It was too hard to say.

CHAPTER TWENTY-FIVE

FOR THE FIRST time since I started riding, I didn't go to the stables the next morning. I would've gone if I could've just snuck in to see Chance, but I knew I'd run into everybody else. Just didn't feel like dealing with it, so I told Pops I didn't feel good.

"Thought you were serious about riding," he said.

"I am, but my stomach's acting up." I folded my hands over the front of my shirt like I was holding something in.

"Does your not feeling good have anything to do with the party?"

"Maybe I ate something I shouldn't have," I said, heading back upstairs to my room. I couldn't tell him how I'd messed everything up again.

I stayed there for a little bit but I got tired of hiding out, so I went outside to sit on the porch. Mr. Glover must have heard the screen door close 'cause he looked up from sweeping his front steps. After he finished, he took his time cleaning the sidewalk before coming over to our house.

"Stables must be closed today," he said, leaning on his broom.

"Stables open. I'm sick."

"I see. What about your horse? Chance—is that her name? Wonder who's taking care of her this morning."

What was it about Mr. Glover? He had a way of making me feel like a chump without coming right out and saying it.

I slumped over in my chair, trying to look sick. "She'll be all right. There's other kids who can cover."

"What about your dad?"

"What?"

"Your dad. He borrowed money from your uncle Ronnie to buy you those riding boots."

Mr. Glover wasn't a doctor. How'd he know I wasn't sick? And Pops never told me he had to borrow the money for all my riding gear.

"Let's hope you feel better tomorrow," he said. "Otherwise, I may have to go over there and take care of Chance myself."

"You, mucking out a stall? It's not easy like sweeping the sidewalk."

Mr. Glover straightened up. He was holding the broom by his side like a sword. "What makes you think keeping this block clean is easy?"

I'd never seen Mr. Glover mad, but he looked pretty close to it. The thing is, he made taking care of the block look easy. He looked like he enjoyed sweeping the sidewalks, cleaning the gutters, and shoveling snow, even in front of the abandoned houses. He kept the block together. Always calling the city to complain about things that weren't right.

"If something's yours, you gotta take care of it," he said, turning to see who was pulling into an open parking spot a few doors down. He went over to say hello.

I knew I needed to be with Chance. Everything bad disappeared when I was with her. I had to get over to the stables, but Pops would guess something was up. First I was sick, then I wasn't. Whatever. I couldn't wait until tomorrow to see my horse.

I opened the screen door and looked into the living room. Pops was sitting in his recliner, reading the paper. He had his music on. He looked up when I opened the door.

"How are you feeling?" he mouthed over the music, putting the paper down.

"A lot better." I bent over to touch my toes. You know, trying to show that everything was working again.

"Be back at the stables tomorrow?"

"Yeah, um, I could even go today."

"What'd you say?" He turned the music down so we could hear each other.

"I'm thinking of going to the stables this afternoon," I said. "It's not really fair to stick the other kids with my work."

"Sure you're up to it?"

"Yeah, I miss Chance," I said.

"Okay." He went back to his paper. "See you at dinner."

The music was back up the way he liked it when I brought the bike through the living room. I waved at him before heading out.

I was used to riding over to the stables in the morning when everything was quiet. Now everybody was outside and they were loud. Like the bunch of little kids playing at the open fire hydrant. They sprayed me with their water guns when I rode past.

Maybe I would get lucky and not see anybody who'd been at Alisha's party. The one thing on my side was that it was late. Some of the kids would have gone home already. I wanted to tell Winston and Alisha I was sorry while nobody else was around.

Riding through Fairmount Park, I smelled a million barbecues. Well, it was the end of June. I was in the park every day but I didn't notice all these folks out here enjoying themselves. Maybe I didn't really want to.

CHAPTER TWENTY-SIX

THE STABLES WERE QUIET when I rolled up on my bike. This was different from the morning hustle I was used to. It was hot and the air wasn't moving. Most of the horses were standing together in the shady part of the yard, stamping their feet and flicking their trails, trying to chase the flies away.

It took a few minutes for my eyes to adjust to the light in the barn. Just looking at the pitchforks and smelling that horse smell made me feel better. Hadn't even seen Chance yet. She wasn't in the stables. Nobody was, as far as I could see.

I saw something move, though, out of the corner of my eye. Percy. He didn't come over to me. Me and him weren't close 'cause I always got hung up on how he looked. Just stupid, I guess. He wasn't different from Chance, really. Watching me, waiting to see what I was gonna do. I went over and pet him a little bit. I hoped he wasn't hurt. I added water to his bowl just to be sure he had enough.

Instead of going out the front, I took the side door. It would be easier to look for Chance behind the barn that way. She was there. She was dripping water 'cause somebody had just hosed her down. That's what I usually did.

"Boy, am I glad to see you," I said. She nickered and moved her ears forward when she heard my voice.

I went back inside the barn and got a sweat scraper. I was scraping the water off of her when somebody came up behind us.

"Glad you could make it." It was Winston.

"I'm sorry," I said, still working on Chance.

"Sorry for what? For fighting, for not showing up, for what?" He walked around Chance so we were facing each other.

"I wasn't fighting," I said, still not looking at him. "Jerome's the one who crashed into the table."

"Well, we all agree on at least one thing," he said. "Jerome fell into the table but he says you tripped him, intentionally."

"I didn't trip nobody. He fell over that girl's shoes."

"He's not here to dispute you, now is he?" Winston's voice was tired. "For your information, Jerome's hurt pretty badly. Besides spraining his ankle, he also hurt his shoulder. That's bad news for a polo player."

Neither one of us said anything. I'd finished drying off Chance but I kept my hand on her.

"What am I supposed to do with you?" Winston said, stepping back and leaning up against the barn. "You say one thing; Jerome says another. The truth is probably somewhere in between." Winston sighed. "Jerome's not nice. I know that. I thought I could build a powerhouse polo team, but my two best horsemen trying to kill each other."

"I ain't try to kill nobody," I said. "Told you he tripped on that girl's shoes." Chance was shifting her weight on her back legs. She wasn't any more comfortable than I was. I wanted Winston to just disappear so I could be alone with my horse.

"What makes this so hard is that I like you," he said.

"Yeah, why's that?" I was petting Chance with both hands now. She was snuggling her head into my chest. I could swear she was telling me to fess up. Admit I tripped Jerome.

"You don't give up," he said. "I had a hard time fitting in when I first started riding, too. Took me a while to figure out that it was my own fears holding me back."

Well, he probably didn't have no cops jumping on him in the street. I wondered how he would've handled that. Both me and Chance were nervous. If he was going to suspend me, I wished he'd just hurry up and do it.

"But it wouldn't be fair to suspend you and not Jerome," he said. "Unless you really did trip him."

I couldn't look at Winston. Just shook my head no with

my hands on Chance's neck. Winston looked at me and Chance for a long minute. I don't know if he really believed me, but he knew that losing Chance would've done me in.

"Okay," he said, sighing again, "let's get back to your training."

I nodded, still holding on to Chance. Winston walked back into the barn. "See you in the morning," he said over his shoulder.

I WAS STILL HOLDING CHANCE when I got a text. I thought it was Winston trying to tell me some polo stuff but it was Alisha.

Call me. That's all it said.

I wasn't trying to play her off, but I wanted to just be alone with the horses. I led Chance down the aisle in the barn, stopping to say hello to Luke and Magic.

"Jerome will be all right," I said, leading Chance into her stall. "He started the whole thing." She nuzzled my shoulder as I turned her around to face the front of her stall.

I called Alisha but she didn't answer, so I left a message. "Hey, Alisha," I said. "First off, I want to say I'm real sorry about how your party ended up. It wasn't my fault, though. Jerome's the one who fell into the table. I saw Winston a little while ago. Me and him are cool. I'm with Chance now."

I checked Chance's water bucket before closing her stall door. "See you tomorrow," I said.

Then I got another text from Alisha. I read it out loud. *Don't leave i need to see u.* Chance pricked up her ears. "I guess we'll just wait to see what she wants," I said.

We didn't have to wait long. Alisha came into the barn, carrying her saddle. She put her stuff away in the tack room and marched right over. She started petting Chance, hardly looking at me. Chance liked Alisha. I could tell by the way she had her ears cocked in her direction.

"What's up?" I said.

Alisha sighed but she still didn't look at me. "Troy, I know you think you got over . . . but I know you tripped Jerome."

"He fell . . ." I started saying, but she held up her right hand.

"Don't worry. I'm not going to tell anybody." She turned to look at me then. "Just like I didn't tell anybody about you kicking Percy."

"I only kicked Percy once," I said. "How many times do I have to tell you that?"

"You need to get a grip!" she shouted. Chance's ears twitched and she switched her tail. "Now look what you've made me do," said Alisha, sighing again. "We're scaring Chance."

She was the one scaring Chance. "Let's go outside," I said. She didn't move at first, but I started walking away. If she was gonna holler again, she could have all the horses in here upset. We walked to the front of the barn to the same spot where we'd seen that hawk.

Alisha took a third deep sigh. "Troy, you're not the only one who's ever had problems with the cops." I tried to wave her away. "I know you don't want to hear this, but you better listen." I was just standing there, leaning up against the wall.

"I, for one," she said, "know the cops better than you ever will."

"I doubt that."

"Just listen," she said. "I had a real hard time when my parents died. Hanging out with some mean kids, not going to school . . ."

I rolled my eyes and looked up at the sky. She went on.

"The worst was when I was stealing stuff. That's when Uncle Winston brought me to Philly to live with him. He knew that being with the horses would help straighten me out."

"You got caught shoplifting?" I said. "That's how you got in trouble with the cops?"

She nodded.

"Alisha." This time I had to sigh. "You got caught doing something wrong. The cops jumped me for walking down the street." Her head jerked back like she didn't know that before. "Now, tell me, what's wrong with that?"

She closed her eyes. "Why can't you just get over it?" she said, shaking her head.

I looked at her standing there with her eyes closed. She thought she knew everything but this was something she just didn't get.

"Because," I said. "Because, I'm afraid . . ." I stopped 'cause my throat started tightening up. "I'm afraid it's going to happen again." I hadn't even admitted that to myself.

She opened her eyes and looked at me. "Well . . . maybe you can . . . move."

I laughed. "I don't have a rich uncle who can just swoop in and take me away."

"It wasn't like that." She twisted her mouth to one side. "Uncle Winston didn't swoop in. He had to leave the polo circuit to take care of me."

Maybe me and Alisha weren't meant to get any closer. The thought hit me right in my face when she said that. I mean, I knew she had a nice life. A life that was different from mine, but all those brick walls around her house prevented her from seeing what was happening on the other side. It felt like one of those walls was standing between us.

"I'm telling you all this 'cause you aren't the only one who's had to deal with bad things," she said. "So do what you gotta do, but . . . you need to know I don't think it's cool. You need to stop lying."

I jammed my hands into my pockets and squeezed my eyes shut. Felt like Alisha was asking me to choose between her and Chance. Chance understood me; Alisha didn't. Maybe she never would.

CHAPTER TWENTY-SEVEN

THE NEXT FEW WEEKS flew by. Everybody knew I was gonna play in exhibition, especially since Jerome was out. Sounded like he was pretty messed up. He didn't need surgery or nothing like that, but between his ankle and his shoulder, he had to rest for a whole month. Winston told me that. Everybody was wondering if he'd be back before the end of the summer. Alisha was the only person who knew how Jerome really got hurt. Girl must have been psychic. Or maybe she had superpowers where she could see in the dark. I never asked her how she knew. She just did. She was acting cold 'cause I didn't tell anybody what really happened. Wasn't any need to rock the boat.

I was riding Chance every morning and doing polo in the afternoons. Winston had me working on my swings in the little barn at the end of the polo field. That's where the wooden horse was. Had to learn the basic strokes on that first. I wanted to be fierce like the players out at Blanchard, hanging off the sides of their horses at full gallop. Well, I couldn't do that yet, but that's what I was going for.

I was in the barn with Dre one afternoon when Miss T and Foster dropped by, looking for Winston. They needed him to sign some papers so Foster's record wouldn't say he'd dropped out of the program.

"Look at you," said Miss T with a big grin. "You're fantastic with that mallet." I was already pretty good at nearside fore and back shots. Had to show off a little bit, so I did the offside shots, too.

"This is harder than it looks," I said. I had on my brown leather boots and gloves, looking a little bit like Winston. I wondered if Foster was sorry he wasn't training with me.

"You look good." Foster nodded as he watched my little performance. If he was jealous, he did a real good job of hiding it. "I saw you and Chance coming up off of the trail last week. Your flow was tight."

"Oh, he's definitely on it," said Dre. "No question about that."

"Yeah, this is my thing," I said.

It was true. I felt good even on the wooden horse, and that was nothing compared to riding. Jerome wasn't around, so I could just be myself and not worry about who was scared of me, who was trying to take me down, nothing like that. Miss T went off to find Winston.

"When will you move off this wooden thing and play polo on a real horse?" Foster asked.

"Pretty soon. Have to learn how not to knock myself upside the head first," I said, dismounting from the wooden horse. I used to hold the mallet all crazy. Now I knew to hold it down below my waist with other people around. I didn't know what else to say, so I asked about that girl he'd met at Alisha's party.

"How's Niki?" I said. Me and Dre were walking around the barn, picking up my practice balls.

"Everything's cool." Trying to hide his grin, Foster walked over to the corner and took a mallet out of the barrel. Fooling around with it gave him something to do. I never saw my boy like this. He was all lit up. Pops used to look like this when he was around my mom.

"Might be going to a barbecue at her crib on Saturday." He was still fooling with the mallet, not looking at me.

"So you're going back down to Society Hill?" We'd found all my practice balls. My pockets were stuffed with them.

"No, they live around Rittenhouse Square."

"Didn't we drive past there with Miss T?"

"Yeah." He put the mallet back in the barrel.

"So, let me get this straight," I said. "You don't like people out at Blanchard, but Rittenhouse Square is okay?"

He shrugged. Dre was taking the saddle off the wooden horse but he stopped and looked at me.

"This what you came to tell me?" I asked.

"Just came to check you out," he said.

"Well, check you out," I mumbled under my breath.

"Huh?" Foster said.

"Guess I ain't no girl," I said through tight lips.

"And I ain't no horse," he said, swallowing hard.

Dre looked like he was sorry he was there. Felt like all the air was sucked out of the barn. Me and Foster were standing right next to each other but there was a big space between us.

"Okay, look," Dre said. "I know this isn't my business, but you need to listen to yourselves. You've been friends forever; you're practically brothers." His face was wide open like he didn't have any secrets. "There's nothing wrong with friends developing different interests. Just give each other some room. That's all."

The truth was I missed Foster. The problem was, I couldn't say it. I couldn't say it 'cause he knew who he was way more than I did. He wasn't following anybody else's rules, not mine, not anybody's.

"Well, I hope Niki's pops ain't like Winston," I said, trying to make a joke about the whole thing. I thought Foster would pick up on it and do his Winston imitation.

"Don't worry," he said. "I can handle it if he is." He just said it flat like that. The thing is, I knew Foster could handle whatever came his way. Foster's quick on the uptake. He's totally like that.

CHAPTER TWENTY-EIGHT

FOSTER SAID HE wasn't a horse. I never said he was. I asked Chance about it the next morning when we were out on our ride.

"First off," I said, "Foster only has two legs and you have four." I knew Chance was listening 'cause she had one ear cocked. "And you have more muscles than he does." I said that even though Foster had filled out from all the work he'd done earlier in the summer. "But maybe he's mad 'cause you're a girl, just like I could get mad 'cause he's all wrapped up with Niki." Chance just kept going. I didn't expect her to answer, but it still felt good to tell her everything. "Well," I said, "I'm not gonna worry about it. Like he said, he's got his own stuff."

I was totally into my training after that. Winston finally moved me up from the wooden horse to practicing polo swings on Chance. Then, one morning, Winston brought Willie and Little Keith to watch me practice.

"I wanted these guys to see how well you're doing," Winston said, nodding to them. I'd never been around the other polo players without Jerome, so I didn't know what to expect.

Little Keith was quiet but Willie was straight up. "You got big shoes to fill," he said. "Marcus moving away and now Jerome, well, you know."

"When's Jerome coming back?" I asked. Willie exchanged a look with Little Keith but they didn't answer.

"That's still an open question," said Winston. "His ankle's coming along nicely but the shoulder is going to need more time."

"Yeah, screwing up your shoulder ain't funny," said Willie. He lifted his right arm and swung it over his head. "I definitely don't want anybody messing with this."

"Let's just see how it goes," said Winston. "But you're right, Willie. This couldn't have happened at a worse time. We were already one man down."

"Well," Willie said, looking at me, "let's see what you got."

I already had Chance tacked up, so I swung myself up into the saddle. I was holding the reins in my left hand, you know, like you do in polo, and Winston handed me the mallet on the right side.

"Good, good, you're doing everything right," he said. He'd spent a lot of time talking about how dangerous polo was. It was real important to do things right.

"Okay, warm her up like I showed you," he said. Me and Chance made slow canter circles to the right. "Start your circle taps. I wanna see you tap ten times without missing the ball."

So, there I was, riding Chance and tapping the ball with half-swing shots to the right. There was a lot of stuff to remember. How to move up and down in the saddle, squeeze your knees, turn your shoulders, keep your head over the ball, and look at it before you swing. Winston had me practice stuff like that over and over. Even had me riding without stirrups so I could learn how to stay on Chance without them.

Willie said something I couldn't hear to Winston and Little Keith. Winston nodded, but Little Keith still didn't say anything. "Right, Keith?" Willie said. Little Keith just shrugged.

I finished my little routine and dismounted.

"Not bad," said Willie.

"I told you he was good," said Winston, smiling as I walked toward them. "I've never seen a beginner take to this so quickly."

"Reminds me of Jerome," said Little Keith. "He took to this real quick, too. I sure hope he's all right."

Nobody said anything. You could've cut the silence with a knife.

"I'm gonna take care of Chance," I said, walking her around to the hose. Winston nodded. I was glad to get away. Felt like they knew I was the cause of Jerome's getting hurt. And there were two of them; I was alone.

CHAPTER TWENTY-NINE

"CAN YOU GIVE ME A HAND with these boxes?" Dre was standing at the bottom of the stairs leading up to his apartment. Looked like he'd thought he could carry both boxes himself but, after just one step, realized they were too heavy.

"Sure," I said, taking the top one and following him up to his place.

Most of the horses were outside the barn, so we didn't have them right under our feet but you could still hear their sounds coming through Dre's open windows.

"Do you ever have parties up here?" I asked. Didn't seem like it'd be a good idea to have pumping music and folks dancing so close to the horses.

"Just get-togethers," he said, setting down his box and motioning for me to do the same. "I used to have the polo team over, but not so much this summer." He didn't have to say why that was. "You and Foster should come and sleep over before school starts. You know, see what it's really like to live out here in the park."

"I don't think Foster would dig it," I said.

"Hmm." He'd opened the refrigerator and held up a pitcher of lemonade, asking if I wanted a glass. I nodded and he poured some for each of us.

"Me and Foster aren't really hanging out," I said, taking the cool glass from his hand. "You know, he's not riding anymore and he's into that girl, Niki."

"And you?" Dre said between gulps of lemonade. "Are you hanging with anybody?"

"I'm into the horses," I said, shrugging. It was real easy to talk to him, so I added, "Me and Alisha were getting tight but, I don't know, something happened . . ."

"Are you cool with that?" he said.

"Not really, but, you know . . ."

"Don't let it slip away, man," he said. "I know you're down with the horses and all, but you need human friends, too."

I put the glass on Dre's table and picked up one of his horse magazines. "I was with Jerome's boys today."

Dre's eyes widened. "Willie and Little Keith?"

"Well," I said, "I wasn't really hanging with them. Winston brought them around to watch me practice."

"And . . ."

"It was okay, except I get the feeling everybody's mad about what happened to Jerome."

"I'm not gonna lie and tell you they're not," he said, "Winston's real disappointed. You know, he's all about the polo." Dre hesitated for a second. "Sometimes a little too much, but things happen."

"Jerome fell," I said, looking down at the floor.

"That's not hard to do at Winston's place." Dre gathered some papers off the table. "I've slipped over there myself. He needs to replace those bricks."

"When's Jerome coming back?" I said.

Dre shrugged. "Nobody knows for sure." He rolled the papers up and put a rubber band around them. "You cool?" he said, looking at me. I nodded and put the magazine back on the table. "Let me come down with you," he said. "I need to check on everything before my buddies come over to watch the game."

We walked back down to the ground floor. Dre didn't lecture me any more about what he thought I should do. He'd already said his piece and, being cool like he was, he left it at that.

CHAPTER THIRTY

GRANDMOM MAKES A real good mac and cheese. We had it for dinner that night and Uncle Ronnie came over with some cherry vanilla ice cream, my favorite. Usually, I'm all over it, but I stopped after I ate the two scoops Grandmom dished out.

"Uh-oh," said Uncle Ronnie, looking at Pops, "something's up. Troy's not fighting me over this ice cream."

"I'm in training," I said, pushing back from the dining room table.

"That never stopped you before." Uncle Ronnie leaned on his right elbow, waving his spoon in my direction.

"Elbows off the table," said Grandmom before adding, "Maybe he's had enough. Nothing wrong with that."

I wanted to excuse myself from the table and go up to my room, but they would have questioned that, too. I'd started thinking on my way home from the park. What would happen if I told the truth to just one person? Like Pops or Mr.

Glover. I thought about it some more. Pops wasn't a good choice. He'd make me tell Winston for sure and who knows what would happen then. I'd probably get suspended or even kicked out. Mr. Glover wouldn't work, either. He'd just make me feel bad about lying. Foster was the one. He wouldn't tell anybody. Well, I don't know, maybe he'd tell his girlfriend, Niki. I definitely wasn't feeling that. Plus, I'd have to go find him. I still wasn't ready to do that, either.

"The exhibition match is coming up. Maybe it's just jitters," said Pops. He'd been looking almost like his old self the past few weeks. He was back into his music and telling everybody about me.

"I might bring a date," said Uncle Ronnie. "You should see the attention I get from the ladies when I tell them my nephew plays polo."

Grandmom rolled her eyes. "Leave it to you to find new ways to get dates."

Pops was laughing down at his end of the table. "Is that why you were so eager to loan me the money for Troy's gear?" He caught my eye and winked.

"No," Uncle Ronnie said, staring down at his plate. He wiped his mouth with his napkin. "I knew this would be a good thing for Troy . . . for all of us." We looked at him. He wasn't being funny or talking about ladies.

Pops leaned across the table and touched Uncle Ronnie's arm. "You were right about that and I thank you. I'm only sorry Troy's mom isn't here to see him now." This was the first time in a year he'd mentioned my mom without looking real bad.

"Well, I'm proud of all of you," said Grandmom, getting up from her chair. She walked around the table and kissed Uncle Ronnie on the forehead.

All of this because of me. I licked my lips and took a deep breath. How could I tell the truth now and mess everything all up again?

CHAPTER THIRTY-ONE

ALL EVERYBODY WAS talking about was exhibition. Winston's team won last year and he wanted to do it again. He was totally obsessed with it.

Me, I was practicing every day with Willie, Little Keith, and Marcus since his parents let him stay in Philly with his aunt until the end of the summer. He'd be our fourth player if Jerome wasn't back in time.

Two weeks had passed since I thought about telling the truth to somebody but, I don't know, Pops and everybody were happy. It didn't seem right to spoil that. That's what I told myself. Anyway, I was up in my room after dinner one night when somebody knocked on my bedroom door. I thought it was Pops or Grandmom.

"It's open," I yelled.

I didn't get up off the bed 'cause I thought one of them would just stick their head in. It was Foster. We always used to get together at his house. I don't remember how that got started; it just was. This may have been the first time he was in my room in like five years.

"Yo, man, come on in." I sat up and put down the book I was reading.

"Don't tell me," he said, walking over to see what the book was. "You're reading about polo."

"Yup, gotta be on my game, cuz." I swung my legs off the bed and pointed to the desk chair behind him. He pulled it out and straddled it.

"Well, that's what I came to talk to you about," he said. "Jerome's coming back to the stables."

"How do you know that?"

"Miss T told me."

"Miss T? How does she know?"

Foster looked down at the floor. "You were right about Miss T and Winston."

"What?" I fell back on my bed.

"Yup," he said. "He calls her every night and he's taking her out this weekend."

"Where? Where are they going?" I don't know why, but I wanted to know where Winston hung out.

"I don't know," he said. "They're still working on it." Foster's shoulders slumped. "It's weird to have my mom going on dates," he said.

"Maybe she won't like him or maybe she won't be able to stand his homies."

"My mom can handle herself with anybody . . . if she wants to." That was true. Foster got that from her. He shrugged. "We'll see how you feel when your pops starts going out."

I wasn't ready for that. I changed the subject so I wouldn't have to think about it.

"So when did Miss T tell you about Jerome?"

"Today. Winston's gonna talk to you tomorrow." He hesitated before adding, "I figured you could use a heads-up."

I fiddled with the book I'd just put down. Everybody thought I was the cool one but it was Foster who had guts. He was still looking out for me and he wasn't afraid to let me know it.

"Yeah, thanks, man," I said, but I knew that wasn't enough. He took a big step in coming over here. "Thanks for watching my back. No horse can do that."

"What?" he said. "Chance can't do everything?"

"I'm not saying all that." I held my hands up. "But, you know, we go way back; nothing's gonna change that."

I didn't say anything else for a minute 'cause I didn't want to get all sloppy, but I knew I had to tell him what really happened at Alisha's party.

"Jerome may still be mad about the party," I said.

"Then he should be mad at that girl with the big shoes."

"No, he shouldn't," I said. "I'm the one who tripped him."

Foster's mouth fell open. "For real?" he said.

I nodded. "He made me mad when he started laughing at me in front of everybody."

"Nobody could tell you did it," he said. "It was too dark."

"I know, but Jerome felt it."

"What are you gonna do?" he asked.

"I'm gonna watch him like a mug. What do you think?"

"I mean, besides that." He thought for a few minutes. "Nobody thinks we talk anymore. Maybe I can wear a recorder and catch him saying something bad about you."

My boy always was into that detective stuff. He had all these ideas about putting cameras in the tack room and even in the horse stalls. The thing is, he didn't put me on the spot about not telling him about all of this before. I guess he missed me as much as I missed him. He was just more honest about it.

We talked about Jerome until there wasn't nothing else to say. That's when I asked him about his girlfriend. He started grinning before I could even get her whole name out. I just said, "Ni," and that's all it took. Turns out, he did go to her crib. Turns out, her people were nice. Turns out, she was his girl. We talked about that until it was almost ten o'clock.

"Yo, man," I said, "I know you're hooked up and everything, but Miss T's gonna be mad if you're late."

I was laying on my bed, looking straight up at the ceiling. Winston dating Miss T. I wondered if he would try to get her into horses.

"Is Miss T gonna start riding?"

"I don't know," he said. "Probably. She likes to try new things."

I lifted my head and arched my eyebrows at Foster. "Better watch out, man. Before you know it, you're gonna be getting a horse for Christmas."

Foster had one hand on the doorknob, but he stopped and flicked dirt off his sleeve. He looked at his wrist like he was checking his watch. "Pony, never horse," he said. Cracked me up.

CHAPTER THIRTY-TWO

TRUTH IS A FUNNY THING. I mean, sometimes it's okay to tell a little lie so nobody gets their feelings hurt. Like Grandmom's mac and cheese was a little off that night she kissed Uncle Ronnie, but I still said it was good. And was it a lie to let Dre think Jerome fell because of Winston's wet bricks? Dre said he'd slipped at Winston's house before.

I talked all this over with Chance on our ride the next day. She was glad I had Foster back in my corner even if he wasn't all into her like I was. That was okay. Me and Chance both knew I was real lucky to have him as a friend.

Winston called me into his office when I got back to the barn. "Watching you with these animals reminds me of Jerome," he said. "He'll be back tomorrow, you know."

I didn't let on that I'd already heard the news. "So, he's okay?"

"Yes, thank goodness. He's fine."

"Well, I'm cool," I said, "but I can't speak for him."

"I've spoken with him several times since he's been out," said Winston. "He just wants to get back to his training."

I nodded to signal I felt the same way.

"I'm going to tell you the same thing I told him." He paused here so his words would sink in. "Any trouble and you're out. You got that?"

"I hear you," I said.

"All right." He looked relieved that he'd gotten that out of the way.

I was getting up to leave when Alisha knocked on Winston's door. She came in without waiting for him to answer.

"Oh, I'm sorry," she said, "I didn't know you had anybody with you."

"It's okay," said Winston. "What's on your mind?" Alisha lowered her eyes. "Don't try to act shy now," he teased.

"I just ran into Dre and he told me Jerome's coming back."

"That's right," said Winston. "Me and Troy were just talking about it."

Alisha cut her eyes at me. "Well, uh . . . are you still going to need Marcus for exhibition? I know he was ready to substitute."

"Probably not," said Winston. "He was willing to help us out, but his family's already moved away." Winston looked at his watch and stood up. "I have somebody coming for a lesson," he said. "Is that all you wanted to ask me?"

Alisha gave her uncle a weak smile.

"Okay," he said. "Don't keep Troy too long. He's still got a lot of work to do."

We heard him whistling as he walked out to meet his student. Alisha leaned up against the wall behind Winston's desk.

"What's the good word?" I said.

"That's what I was going to ask you."

"Chance is cool," I said, shrugging. "I'm getting ready for exhibition . . ."

"You still, you know, keeping everything to yourself?" She looked a little bit sad. Like, maybe, she missed being friends.

"No," I said. "I took your advice. I talked to somebody about it."

"That's good," she said. "It's not good to keep bad stuff to yourself."

"Yeah, well, Foster understood the whole thing."

"Foster," she said. "That's the only person you told?" She sat down in Winston's chair and put her head in her hands. "Troy, you're still trying to get over. You need to be straight up with Uncle Winston or Dre, somebody like that."

"Can't do it," I said, looking out the window. "They'll kick me out."

"You don't know that," she said. "They understand everything you've been through."

"What have I been through, Alisha?" I turned around so we were looking at each other. "First my mom dies and then the cops jump me. Do you know how that feels?"

"I don't know how it feels to be jumped, but I know about the other part." She sat back in Winston's chair and looked up at the ceiling. "Both of my parents are dead, Troy. Did you hear me? Both of them." She sat there breathing real hard. "Remember I told you it gets better?" She closed her eyes and one little tear streamed down her face. "That wasn't a lie. It's true, it does get better, but sometimes . . . sometimes I still catch myself crying. And the problem is, I don't know which one of them I'm crying for."

"Probably both," I said.

"What?" She opened her eyes and wiped the tear off her chin.

"You're probably crying for both of them . . . and for yourself."

"I think you're crying for yourself, too," she said. "You just don't want to admit it." She stood up and pushed Winston's chair close in under his desk. "But you're losing yourself in your hard feelings."

"I can handle the hard feelings."

"Right." She gave a little laugh. "Just what we need around here, another person who's mad all the time."

"I can handle Jerome, too," I said.

"I sure hope so, Troy. I really, really do."

• • •

I TOOK A detour going home that day. Just wanted to spend more time in the park by myself. Fairmount Park. It was more a part of me than ever before. I watched the little yellow birds with black wings darting in and out of the bushes. Felt like even they were asking me when I was going to let the bad stuff go.

Alisha was right. I didn't want to be hard anymore. If I stayed hard, it would mean the cops had won. They'd tried to make me feel small that night out on the sidewalk but they couldn't stop everything I had going for me. Only I could do that if I let the hardness take over. Well, that's not how I wanted to flow. That's not what my mom had loved about me. That's not what I loved about myself.

CHAPTER THIRTY-THREE

JEROME. JEROME PLAYED IT COOL the next day. He stopped at the barn door, adjusting his eyes to the dim light before stepping inside. I was busy getting Chance tacked up for our practice but I know he saw me. He went through the barn with Winston, saying hello to all the horses before he worked his way over to where I was.

"Hey, man," I said. "Everything good?"

"Good as gold," he said. "That's the gold we could win if this exhibition game was the Olympics."

"That's the right attitude," said Winston. "Give every game everything you've got."

We were standing near Dre's Star bulletin board and Jerome walked over to check it out. Marcus had written a rap about how he wasn't going to miss mucking out the stalls. That was at the top of the board. Under that were pictures of me, Willie, and Little Keith on our horses and beside that Dre had tacked up a *Welcome Back, Jerome* note.

Jerome gave a low *humph*. "I see you worked your way up on the board," he said. He wasn't looking directly at me but I could tell his mouth was set real tight. It hadn't taken him even a half an hour to start in.

"Look," I said. "Maybe we can change things up now that you're back."

"How's that?"

"We can start by talking about the party," I said. I threw it right out there 'cause I didn't want to have to spend all my time worrying about it. I even caught Winston by surprise on that one. He drew his head away and his eyes darted back and forth between Jerome and me.

Jerome hesitated for a few seconds. "Nothing to talk about," he said. "I'm over that."

He walked back down the aisle to Magic's stall and started getting her ready for practice. Everybody knew you really had to be on your game to control her. There were other horses he could have ridden on his first day back but he chose her. To be real, it was a big deal for me to be training with him. He could do figure eights at a gallop and stuff like that.

I had Chance ready to go, so I started leading her out of the barn over to the polo field. Winston followed along.

"Smart of you to clear the air," he said. "I think you and Jerome are going to be okay."

That's what he was wishing for. I wasn't so sure that was how things were going to play out. Jerome rode by us on

Magic and took her around the field a few times while we watched.

"Okay, Troy," Winston said. "Your last few solo sessions have been great. Why don't you guys do some two-rider drills?"

"Definitely," I said.

"Ready, Jerome?" Winston called across the field.

"Sure." He rode over to where we were standing.

I mounted Chance so me and Jerome were both on our horses.

"Troy, this'll be more practice for learning how to look behind you to see where the other rider hits the ball and then joining the line to take the next shot," Winston explained.

So I went up and down the field with Jerome all morning. I'd tap the ball up the field and then ride past it, leaving it for him to hit up to me. I had to keep looking behind me after I passed the ball so I could see where he was hitting it. Jerome gave me pointers like us riding together was no big deal, like everything was cool between us. My neck started to hurt after a while, so we took a break.

"Shoulder holding up?" Winston called to Jerome when he saw us stopping.

Jerome gave him a thumbs-up. "Troy needs a break," he said.

We walked Chance and Magic over to the water buckets. We didn't really know what to say to each other, so I did some neck circles while the horses were drinking. Chance brought her head up out of her bucket and just sorta nudged me. Maybe that's what made me come out with it.

"Look, man," I said. "About Alisha's party . . ."

Jerome frowned, surprised that I was bringing the party up again. "I'm past that," he said.

"Well, I'm not." Chance nudged me with her head again. "Look . . . I'm sorry things went down the way they did. I shouldn't have tripped you."

Jerome's nostrils flared like he definitely wasn't expecting to hear that. He stood there patting Magic for a few seconds. "So . . . what? You want a medal or something for telling the truth?"

"No," I said. "I just want to be straight up."

He patted Magic for a few more seconds. "Okay . . ." he said.

Since I'd gone that far it felt like I should put everything out there. You know, just cut through all the mess.

"How's your cousin?" I said. "How's Lay-Lay?"

"What?"

"I know you used to live around the way, and you and Lay-Lay are family."

"Wondered how long it'd take you to figure that out," he said with a smirk. "Okay, yeah, me and Lay-Lay are related but that's about it. We don't hang and I don't plan on changing that. He's not going anywhere; I got plans."

"School like Dre?"

194

"Humph," he said. "I don't know if it's school, but I'm going somewhere."

"Oh, you're gonna be like Winston. Go international and all that—"

"Winston left the circuit," he said, cutting me off. "Nothing's gonna get in my way."

He sounded more than a little uptight but I was just glad to get everything out in the open. Chance nuzzled my shoulder like she was, too.

"All right, you guys," Winston called from the other side of the field. "Break's over."

We went back to our drills. Too bad it took us so long to stop playing games. Maybe we could've been cool from the beginning. Well, it was too late for that, but there wasn't no law saying we couldn't be straight from now on. At least, none that I knew of.

CHAPTER THIRTY-FOUR

POLO'S DIFFERENT FROM OTHER SPORTS. There's all kinds of charges and stuff you can do to make contact with your opponent and stay in his face. It's real physical. That didn't bother any of us, Jerome, Willie, Little Keith, and me. That's right—I was on the team.

I could see Jerome liked to look big. He spent almost as much time grooming himself as he did taking care of the horses. He was bossy and conceited, but he treated me the same as he did the other guys.

Anyway, Winston wanted us to win exhibition, period. I was the new guy on the team, so he spent extra time on my training. That's why he put me on Magic one day. I'd been riding and practicing drills on Chance but Winston said I needed to be comfortable on other horses, too.

Dre and Jerome were outside talking to the dude who takes care of horseshoeing, the farrier, so they saw what went down. See, I knew Magic was going to try to test me and she did. You know, she didn't want to follow my commands at first, but I didn't get mad. Uh-uh. I played like a horse, a horse she couldn't get over on.

"My instincts were spot-on," said Winston. "I knew you could handle her." He looked over at Dre and Jerome. "Did you see that?"

Dre nodded. "Magic's not an easy horse for a new rider to handle," he said.

"Well, I wouldn't say it was easy." I eyed Jerome, who wasn't saying anything.

"Don't be shy," said Winston. "That's not what I need at exhibition."

"I'm going to be on Chance, right?"

"Of course," said Winston. "I just wanted to stretch you a little bit more."

The farrier called Dre's and Jerome's attention back to one of the horses who was having trouble with her hooves, and Winston went with them. I hosed Magic down and dried her off. I felt good 'cause I could handle her. You know, before, I always saw her as the horse that was out of my league. Now everybody saw just how good I was; even Magic was my friend.

CHAPTER THIRTY-FIVE

EVERYTHING WAS GOING RIGHT for a change. Pops was real proud of me and it showed. He fixed up the house and was even planning to have folks over after exhibition. You know, like a postmatch party. Him and Grandmom were fussing about what kind of music to play, jazz or Latin dance; she was serious about her Zumba thing.

Me and my boy Foster hung out when we could. Not always up in his room; sometimes we sat out on his porch 'cause it was cooler. We were out there with Miss T a few days before the match. Me and Foster'd each had two slices of her blueberry pie, so you know we weren't feeling any pain. Grandmom's friend Miss Evelyn was on her way back from the grocery store when she stopped to say hello.

"Good luck on Saturday, Troy. Everybody's rooting for you."

"You're right about that," said Miss T. "Winston's

expecting a nice turnout. I hear even Lay-Lay's coming." She smiled like that was a nice thing.

"Lay-Lay?" I said.

"I heard that, too," said Miss Evelyn, eyeing the last slice of pie. "See, Troy, you even got Lay-Lay excited."

"It's nice to see that," said Miss T. "That child sure needs something." She held her almost empty pie plate out to Miss Evelyn. "Would you like this last slice? I see it's calling out to you." Everybody laughed but I couldn't help but think it was strange that Jerome had invited Lay-Lay. He'd told me they didn't hang.

"Come on inside," said Miss T, holding the door open for Miss Evelyn. "I'll wrap this up for you."

Foster leaned over to me as soon as they were gone. "Are you thinking what I'm thinking?" he said, all dramatic.

"Yeah, Jerome and Lay-Lay. Something about that—"

"Ain't right." Foster finished my sentence.

Miss T would have corrected him if she'd heard him say *ain't*. But even she seemed to think it was nice that Lay-Lay was going to see the match. "Everything's been cool around the stables," I said.

"I don't know," said Foster, shaking his head. "I don't trust either one of them."

"You're starting to sound like me," I said. "I thought I was the one who had trouble with that."

"Well, after what happened with the cops, nobody could blame you for acting weird. Plus, on top of that, you had Jerome making Percy sick 'cause he thought you'd get in trouble for it."

My back stiffened 'cause I'd never told Foster about kicking Percy. "Why'd he think that?"

"'Cause he was looking out Dre's window and saw you kick him." I hadn't seen a window in Dre's apartment, but maybe it was in the back.

"I only kicked him once," I said. "How'd you find all this out anyway?"

Foster's voice was low. "I went over to the stables this morning with Miss T and I heard Jerome talking to Little Keith. They're stupid, man. They just say any old thing without knowing who's around." Foster looked a little hurt. "You should have told me about it, you know, when it happened."

I leaned over to put my paper plate on the floor below my chair. "Yeah, sorry, man."

"Well, I was kinda messed up, too," he said. "I was jealous of Chance . . . still am."

"Chance brings me closer to my mom," I said, looking out over the porch railing. "But . . . so do you."

Foster nodded. "I know, man. I know."

CHAPTER THIRTY-SIX

WE PLAYED EXHIBITION out at Blanchard. Winston could've had it in Fairmount Park but I guess he didn't want to since the park wasn't on the circuit and Blanchard was. The countryside looked different from the way it had in the spring when I'd first gone out there. A lot of green had turned brown in the summer heat. That was on the way to Blanchard. Once we turned off the main road onto the club's long driveway, everything was just as green as it'd been before. Looked like they didn't have to worry about their water bill or nothing like that.

Dre drove our string of horses real slow over all those little winding roads. I wanted Chance in the whole game with me and, since this wasn't a pro match, I could keep her in the game as long as she was in good shape. All the twists and turns in the road made me think about everything that had happened over the summer, but I put that out of my mind. Had to focus on my game.

I was playing the number four spot, defense. We knew the team we were playing, the Wildcats, were strong on offense. They were fast and they could shoot a ball down the field before you even knew they had it. What we needed to do was break up their chance to make goals. That meant I had to be ready for offensive drives and be able to move into position to defend our goal real fast. Once I stopped their attacks, I'd have to get the ball to Jerome, our number three, or up to one of our other players, who would try to score.

I'd been talking to myself a lot. Positive self-talk, that's what it's called. Winston taught me that. *Put all negative thoughts aside and fill your mind with positive energy.* I know, sounds like something Mr. Glover would say, right?

People started coming to the club about an hour before the game. Some were tailgating but a lot of folks just wanted to check out the horses. I looked around for Pops and Grandmom. They were sitting in the bleachers with Foster and Miss T. I recognized them by Grandmom's wide-brimmed hat. There wasn't a VIP tent or anything like that, but it was nice. A bunch of people from our stables were there with Alisha. And Uncle Ronnie was there, too. I had to give it to him; he had a nice-looking lady on his arm.

"Nervous?" Winston asked. I hadn't played at a club like this before. On top of that, it was hot and there wasn't really much of a breeze. We had this sprinkler system hooked up so the horses could stay cool.

"A little," I said. Chance looked pretty good after the ride out from Philly, but I stayed as close to her as I could before the match started.

Blanchard had a really good sound system and they were playing music before the game. This was nothing like our games in the park. Jerome joked that our horses might be too busy eating the nice grass on the polo field to play, but one look over at Magic and Chance told me that wasn't true. Our horses were ready to go.

The Wildcats played at Blanchard all the time and, from the looks of their equipment and horses, they had a lot more money than us. "That's their weakness," said Winston. "They'll be sorry if they don't take us seriously."

Jerome was like the perfect team captain, encouraging all of us to play hard. He even patted me on the back before we rode our horses onto the field for the warm-up. I followed the other players and cantered Chance up and down the field, making a big sweep in front of the bleachers. I don't know who was smiling more, Pops or Grandmom, but I definitely heard Uncle Ronnie yelling, "That's my nephew." It was still hard to believe I was playing polo at Blanchard. Then the music stopped and the starting bell rang. It was time to play.

Jerome won the throw-in and sent the ball crashing down the field. Looked to me like his shoulder was fine. We all tore down the field in a line with equal distance between us, that's how you do it, but we weren't alone. The Wildcats were on us tough. I was right in the middle of it and I was totally wired. My heart was jumping out of my chest and the hair on my arms was standing on end but I never lost my cool, man. I never lost it. I just did what I had to do—paid attention to who was where on the field and how Chance was feeling.

Chance was the key to me making a good showing. I knew that. Felt like she knew it, too. She was coiled underneath me and, I don't know, it just felt like we were flowing together. Real tough.

There was a race between Willie and a Wildcats player and guess who got to the ball first. Willie outgalloped the guy and hit a long pass over to Little Keith. Little Keith worked his way through the horse traffic and, as he got closer to the goal, slowed down to take half hits. He scored. The Wildcats' mouths were just hanging open. We'd totally dominated them.

The ball was thrown in again and this time the Wildcats got control of it and headed for our goal. But, uh-oh, Jerome stole it. He was bad. He knocked it over to me and I did a back shot that sent it down the field, toward the Wildcats goal. The ball went over to the sideboards but Willie chased it down and kept it alive. He made a sprint down the field and just overpowered the Wildcat who was trying to protect their goal. Willie scored. We were totally on our game. The whole first chukka was like that. It ended with us in the lead.

"You guys are working great together!" Winston yelled as we came off the field. "They don't know what hit them." I felt my whole face just beaming. Shoot, I probably looked like Dre or somebody. I even waved at Lay-Lay. He was there talking to Jerome.

Jerome had us doing just what we'd discussed. The Wildcats knew how good he was; they'd seen him play before, so they paid a lot of attention to him. They learned a little too late that they had to pay attention to all of us.

Winston smiled up at me. "You two holding up okay?" He gave Chance water and patted her on her neck and shoulder. "Everything good?"

I nodded and leaned down to whisper to Chance. "You're doing great," I said. She turned her head around to look at me with one of her big brown eyes. She was sweating but she didn't need to come out of the game yet. I rode her back out onto the field with her neck arched and her head held high.

The second chukka started and guess who won the throw-in. Us. The Wildcats were mad now, so they were playing more aggressive. Little Keith shot the ball up to Willie, and the Wildcats were all over him, but Willie outsmarted them. He faked an offside forehand and left the ball where it was. Jerome was right there to pick it up. He worked his way through the horse traffic and exploded down the field. A Wildcat was covering him but he couldn't hang with Jerome. Man, Jerome took it home. He did this mean forehand swing that sent the ball through the goals. Wasn't nothing wrong with his shoulder.

Folks from Philly were standing up in the bleachers, cheering like crazy. Maybe it was that, the wild cheering—whooping and hollering, really—that made something inside me click. That's when I caught fire.

The Wildcats were expecting mostly back shots from me, so they were ready for that. They didn't know how well I could handle the ball. See, they didn't expect me to turn it before I hit it so I could be in more control of where it went. Or, when I did do a back shot, they didn't expect me to hold it until Jerome or Little Keith or Willie was in a better position to receive it.

Put all negative thoughts aside. I kept running that through my head over and over again. Chance felt it. Her ears were standing up like they do when she's alert and, you know, I think mine were, too. Even with the helmet on. Seemed like I heard everything going on around me even before it happened. Like I knew what was coming. I don't know how else to say it. Not only did me and Chance stop the Wildcats from scoring but we turned their attacks into offensive plays for our guys. Me and Chance, we were all over it, man. The Wildcats couldn't break through us. The chukka ended with our team still on top, three to zero.

"Fantastic defense!" Winston yelled. He was beaming from ear to ear and his polo buddies were already coming over to congratulate him.

"Where'd you find your number four?" somebody said. "He can do it all."

"What an asset," somebody else said. "He's stopped the Wildcats dead in their tracks."

Everybody was saying stuff like that. I gulped down some water and closed my eyes to try to calm down.

It was in the third chukka that he got me. Jerome. He was raging, man. The Wildcats won the throw-in but Little Keith and one of their guys were shouting at each other in midfield. All my concentration was on the game but something must have been happening somewhere else, too. The players didn't seem to be where they should be, the refs neither. Me and the number one Wildcat were racing down the field and I could hear Jerome and another player thundering toward us. I got to the ball first and leaned out of my saddle to take a shot. I thought Jerome was going to keep going to receive my pass. Instead, he was heading right for me and Chance. That wasn't right. You can use your pony to bump your opponent's pony but I wasn't his opponent. That's when I saw his face. Totally cold, man. His face was just . . . cold.

I wheeled Chance to the left so she wouldn't get hit full force. Jerome slowed down and turned to the right at the very last second and reached out and yanked me off my horse. Like I said, he was raging. I caught those dead eyes again; there was nothing in them.

I fell real fast but it felt like I was falling in slow motion. Chance turned her head and I looked right into her big brown eye. She watched me go down.

CHAPTER THIRTY-SEVEN

I WOKE UP in the clubhouse. At first, I didn't know where I was 'cause when I opened my eyes the only things I saw were these paintings of horses and dogs. I was in this dark room with wood paneling on the walls and real heavy curtains.

"He's opened his eyes," said Grandmom. She was sitting right beside me on this leather couch. Pops and Uncle Ronnie rushed over from where they were standing with Winston by the window. Alisha was there, too. She was sitting on a couch at the other end of the room with Foster and Miss T.

"What happened?" I said.

"You have a concussion," said Pops, leaning over me. "The club doctor checked you out but we're going to take you to the hospital for observation."

I remembered Jerome charging toward me and Chance but I couldn't remember what happened after that.

"Where's Chance?" I said, trying to get up. "Is she okay?

And Magic?" My head was hurting but I had to know if the horses were all right.

"They're fine," said Pops, holding me by my shoulders. "You know, Chance loves you. She stood over you after you went down."

I sank back down to the couch. "What about the match?"

"They stopped the match after your accident," said Pops.

Winston had been pacing over by the window. He finally stopped and cleared his throat. "It's time to be honest," he said. He walked over to the foot of the couch so I could see him without straining. "Jerome intentionally tried to hurt you and he didn't care if he injured Chance and Magic in the process."

"I can't believe he did this," said Alisha in a quiet voice. She was sitting there with her hands folded in her lap. "He doesn't even care about the horses?"

Winston let out another deep sigh. "It looked to me like Jerome, Little Keith, and Jerome's cousin, what's his name, Lay-Lay, planned the whole thing."

"Lay-Lay again?" said Grandmom.

"Think about it." Winston looked around the room. "Little Keith distracted our attention on the field while Lay-Lay started a commotion in the stands. That gave Jerome the cover he needed to attack Troy. That's what it was, an attack." Winston had on his polo watch. I knew he was nervous 'cause he kept swiveling the face up and down. "I didn't know he was capable of doing something like this."

"He's mad all the time," said Alisha, "but I thought he loved the horses."

"You shouldn't blame yourselves for Jerome's behavior," said Pops.

"No, it's not that simple," said Winston. "I've been obsessed with making a big splash back in the polo world ever since I left it." He looked at all the trophies in the display case. "I was too concerned about having a great team that I could show off out here instead of paying more attention to what was really going on with these kids." He sat down on one of the faded velvet chairs across from the couch. "Maybe I've been pushing them for all the wrong reasons. Maybe it wasn't to help them but just to make me look good."

"You never talked about this," said Miss T. She went over and stood next to Winston's chair. "I wish I had known—"

"You've helped these kids," interrupted Pops. "I can't begin to thank you for what you've done for Troy."

I couldn't look Winston in the face. He was taking the whole thing real hard. That's when I said it. "Jerome got me back for tripping him at Alisha's party."

"Got you back?" Pops frowned.

"I thought me and him were cool after I said I was sorry."

"You apologized to Jerome?" Winston said. "When?"

"On his first day back at the stables. Well, I guess I should have apologized to you, too." I looked up at the ceiling and took a deep breath. "I should be suspended, too."

"Jerome's not suspended," said Winston. "He's out. Same for Little Keith. There's a big difference between tripping somebody and knocking someone off a horse. You could have been killed." Winston shook his head like he was still putting the whole thing together. "And Jerome's cousin came all the way out here to be a part of it. Well, he's in trouble, along with the others."

Uncle Ronnie had been quiet up until then. He sat down and scratched his forehead. "I sure don't like what they did," he said, "but we can't just forget about them."

I looked over at Alisha again. She didn't say anything else. I could tell she was confused from the way she just sat there so quiet. She was smarter than me about some things but she couldn't understand how Jerome and Lay-Lay could be the way they were. So hard that they couldn't be anything else.

"Don't worry," said Winston. "We'll get them some help. I just hope they're open to it."

"That's what I mean," Uncle Ronnie said, pinching the skin at his throat. "Maybe they can turn themselves around."

Nobody said anything else about what I'd done but I knew I couldn't let things stand the way they were.

"I'm sorry I lied," I said.

"I am, too," said Winston. "But don't think for a minute that's what caused Jerome to try to hurt you. He's been jealous of you from the beginning."

"He's the big polo player. What's he got to be jealous of?"

"Heart, Troy." I looked right at Winston then. "You got heart. Jerome's going to be spending a lot of time with his social worker talking about that."

Winston was sitting with his hands hanging over either side of his chair and there was this lamp with a little green shade shining light down on his watch. It finally hit me what was so special about that watch. It was tough enough not to break when it was hit by something hard, but it had another side, too. A soft side that was totally cool. You just had to know when to switch from hard to soft, that's all.

There was a knock on the door and Dre stuck his head inside. "How's everything in here?" His face lit up when he saw that I was awake. "I'll let the horses know you're all right," he said.

All the talking had made me real tired. I sank back into the couch and let my eyelids close without worrying about anything. I didn't need to keep them open to know it was all good.

AUTHOR'S NOTE

HAVE YOU EVER been bitten by a bug? A bug with real sharp teeth that just grabs you and won't let you go? It may not be a bad thing. I'm not talking about real bugs, of course. I'm talking about something that inspires you—a song, a picture, a summer breeze. Anything that inspires you to be creative.

That's what happened to me when I heard about Work to Ride on National Public Radio. Listening to the wonderful story about a mentoring program in Philadelphia's Fairmount Park, where kids get the opportunity to ride horses in exchange for work, was totally inspirational. This was back in 2011 when the Chamounix Equestrian Center's polo team won the US Polo Association's Open National Interscholastic Championship for the first time. Intrigued, I did additional research and found photos of some of the kids. Well, that's what did it. I was bitten by a beautiful bug.

Riding Chance is fiction, but the spark, the idea for it, came from hearing about Work to Ride. Check them out and maybe you'll be inspired, too.

ACKNOWLEDGMENTS

THIS BOOK OWES its existence to my wonderful editor, Andrea Davis Pinkney, who saw a glimmer of a story and encouraged me to write it from the heart; the talented faculty at the Southampton Writers Conference, who embraced me when I needed it most; my New York critique group, who read every word and helped make the pages sing; Elise Arnold and Susie Richards, who introduced me to the world of horses; to Lila Zemborain and the amazing polo player Alberto Bengolea; Miriam Altshuler, agent extraordinaire; and to Rob for his loving encouragement.

ABOUT THE AUTHOR

CHRISTINE KENDALL STUDIED children's literature at the Southampton Writers Conference and was named a semi-finalist in the 2014 River Styx Micro-Fiction Contest. Before becoming an author, Christine worked in the field of law firm talent management. She was honored to join the NAACP Legal Defense & Educational Fund, Inc., to coordinate the fiftieth anniversary commemoration of the historic *Brown v. Board of Education* decision. *Riding Chance* is her first novel. She lives in Philadelphia, Pennsylvania.